MAKING NICE

MAKING NICE

MATT SUMELL

HENRY HOLT AND COMPANY
NEW YORK

Henry Holt and Company, LLC
Publishers since 1866
175 Fifth Avenue
New York, New York 10010
www.henryholt.com

Henry Holt® and 🅗® are registered trademarks of
Henry Holt and Company, LLC.

Some of these stories have appeared elsewhere, in slightly different form: "All Lateral" in *One Story*, no. 200, 2015; "Punching Jackie" in *Electric Literature*'s Recommended Reading, 2015, and in *Noon*, 2009; "Eat the Milk" as "Gift Horse" in *Zyzzyva*, no. 100, 2014, and in *BookGlutton*, 2008; "American Ninja 2" in *Esquire*, January 2013; "Rape in the Animal Kingdom" in *The Esquire Four: New Voices for a New Era of Fiction*, 2012; "Toast" in the *Paris Review*, no. 200, 2012; "OK" in *Electric Literature*, no. 6, 2011; "Little Things" in *Electric Literature*, no. 3, 2010; "Rest Stop" in the *Greenbelt Review*, Spring 2009; "Making Nice" in *Saltgrass*, 2009; "The Block, Twice" in the *Brooklyn Review*, no. 25, 2008; "If P, Then Q" and "Bugs" in *Faultline*, vol. 16, 2007.

Library of Congress Cataloging-in-Publication Data
Sumell, Matt.
    Making Nice / Matt Sumell. — First edition.
        pages cm
    ISBN 978-1-62779-093-2 (hardback) — ISBN 978-1-62779-094-9 (electronic book)
    I. Title.
    PS3619.U456M35 2015
    813'.6—dc23   2014013035

Henry Holt books are available for special promotions and premiums.
For details contact: Director, Special Markets.

First Edition 2015

Printed in the United States of America

10 9 8 7 6 5 4 3 2 1

This book is dedicated to my father, Albert,
who taught me to sail.

CONTENTS

MAKING NICE

Punching
Jackie

Thing is she didn't think that pots and pans should go in the dishwasher, so I pointed out that there's a setting on the dishwasher for pots and pans, just look, it's right there, open your fuckin' eyeballs. Well she didn't like that very much and started in with this business about me being a loser headed nowhere and all that, which normally wouldn't get me going except that it might be true, also 'cause it was coming from someone who supposedly cares about me and who I care about and blah blah blah I mean, I've pretty much looked up to her my whole life—she's been like an older brother to me, but a lady.

Anyway she didn't mean it I don't think, maybe a little, but really it was just her best-guessing what would hurt me most, and I'd be lying if I said I haven't done the same thing myself in arguments past. Just the other night even this girl in a bar was not nice to my nice friend James so I said, "Wow, that's ugly." When she said, "What is?" I said, "Your face.

Now get outta here." It wasn't true, but I was pretty sure it would hurt her feelings, and as it turned out I was correct. I could tell I was correct 'cause she started crying and called me a fuckin' dick, only when she said it, it sounded more like "deck," *fuckin' deck!*—and then she gave me the middle finger and headed off all wiggly-wobbly on her high heels in the direction of the ladies' room.

Also, along similar lines maybe, any racial thing that comes out of my mouth, if not an attempt at humor, is meant only to injure. For example one time this Asian guy was walking extra slow across this crosswalk holding an orange, so I rolled down my window and said, "How about you just pick up the pace a little, Ninjerk. I got places to be and stuff." I didn't mean it, the Ninjerk bit, it's just that he was pissing me off and I wanted to piss him off. I know there's a racial sensitivity there, which minus the modifier is exactly like any other sensitivity: easily exploited. There's no sincerity in it, only malice, which is exactly what I suspect about my sister calling me a loser, except she might've meant it a little. I'm not sure.

Either way it made me upset, and I slammed the refrigerator door so hard the milk exploded, then I turned around and told her to shut it or I'd punch her mustache off her face and watch it fly across the room like a hairy bug. Then I flapped my arms like I was flying, like a bug, like her mustache. Now, I know I crossed a line there, but I hope some people can at least appreciate how much restraint it actually took on my part to not just turn around and haul one off on her. Knowing some people will find that difficult to appreciate, let me employ this awesome analogy: My temper is like a rogue wave of weapons, and my ego is like the dam holding back the rogue wave of weapons from being unleashed on the townspeople/-person, in this case my sister. Sometimes, though, the wave of weapons is too big or powerful or whatever, and some squeeze through a crack or splash over the top or whatever. It's unfortunate, sure, but don't I deserve at least some credit for holding back 99 percent of the entire wave of weapons that I could've just as easily unleashed on her if I wasn't a good person/ego/dam? More important, she was making fun of the ego/dam, provoking it to break or whatever. So in a sense she was sabotaging me, like a fuckin' saboteur. Like a fuckin' dirty, no good, no-pot-washing, dandruff-having lady saboteur. My point, then, is didn't she, in some way, cross a line first? I think so, and *that* is number one on my list of seven excuses as to why it was OK for me to punch my sister in the tits.

1) She started it. I know that's a childish thing to say but . . .

2) When adult siblings revisit the house they grew up in, they often regress back to behaving like children.

3) Sibling status overpowers lady status. Siblings don't count as ladies.

4) Testosterone production has a direct link to aggression and fluctuates in response to competitive situations such as a tennis match or arguments about dishwashers or changes in one's perceived status in a social hierarchy, for example a sibling hierarchy, or a dishwasher-deciding hierarchy, or a *hair*archy of

mustaches (in which case she's the winner hands
down). When disrespected, there is a biological
response within my balls and they make more stuff
that makes more aggression. Try as I might, it's out
of my control. This admittedly may be a weak argument, but the logic is the same as acting like an asshole then blaming it on PMS.

5) There is a certain clarity in violence. There's nothing
rhetorical or vague about it—it means only what it
means, which if I had to I would translate as roughly:
"I don't like you right now, a lot." Less roughly trans-
lated of course depends on the particulars, and considering these particular particulars I'd have to go
with: "The fact that you are insulting me in addition
to being more intelligent, eloquent, calmer, successful,
plus have all your hair and an apartment and a job
that you actually care about frustrates me so greatly
that I am going to dominate you physically because
it's the only area in life in which I think I have the
upper hand." However you translate it, though, it
isn't really all that cruel or enduring. In my experience physical suffering is more transitory than emotional suffering. Words, on the other hand, do lasting
damage. There's no taking them back. Not really.

6) One time I punched a boyfriend of hers in the face
repeatedly because she told me he hit her. Years later
she admitted to me she made it up because she was
mad at him. He died in a car wreck before I could

apologize. Another time this jerk-off in a bar was being a jerk-off to her, and I told him to knock it off. He did, for the most part, and as I made my way back to the table she came running over to me and said, "So-and-So doesn't think you have the balls to hit him." I was younger (dumber) and drunk (extra dumber) and had a canine sense of loyalty, all of which she knew, so I'm sure she figured my reaction would be some version of *Oh yeah?*—which it was. I turned around and walked back over to the guy, tapped him on the shoulder, and slugged him in the ear, et cetera. That makes two out of an approximate forty instances of violence in my life that she in some way instigated, which if my math is correct equals 5-ish percent. My question then is, how can someone who has more than once taken advantage of what I consider brotherly goodwill cry foul when that sort of attention is directed at them? It's all kinds of wrong.

7) She was literally asking for it. After I threatened her she got in my face and yelled, "You think that makes you a big man? Huh? You gonna hit me, *big man?* Well go ahead and hit me then. Hit me. Hit me. Hit me, you fuckin' piece a shit."

"I really want to," I said. "Bad."

"Go ahead then, you fuckin' asshole. You're a fuckin' thirty-year-old fuckin' loser, and you know what else, you fuckin' thirty-year-old fuckin' loser? Mom was right about you, you're a fuckin' abusive piece a shit."

The backstory on that comment is that when our mother was close to dying, she called each of us separately into her hospital room for one last one-on-one conversation—the opportunity to say all the things we'd ever get to say. My sister was called into the room first, and my brother and I waited in the hallway quietly discussing Jennifer, one of the nurses. I told him she was so pretty that I wanted to see her nude, then have sex with her. In so many words he said he wanted the same things, so I told him to back off, but he didn't, so we argued about it. After about ten minutes of this my sister came out looking pretty upset, so we went over and tried our best—which was not good—to comfort her, then asked what it was like. She told us what was said was private, but that overall it was nothing special, mostly a bunch of *I love you*s and *I'm sorry*s and basically amounted to an emotional good-bye. "Sounds tough," I said. "I'm probly gonna have to have unprotected sex with Jennifer in order to deal with all this." As I reached for the door I looked back at my brother and added, "Probly gonna have to suck her gazungas—"

"Mom wants to talk to AJ next," my sister said.

"—I'll lick them. What?"

"Mom wants to talk to AJ next," she repeated.

"That's fine," I lied. And after AJ and I did some overly dramatic nodding at each other, he walked into the room and shut the door behind him. Obviously I was a little bothered by this because I assumed—I think we all did, after Jackie was called in first—that this thing was going down according to birth order, which would mean that I was next in line considering that I was next in line out of our mother, correctly by the way. Headfirst. So when she skipped me it stung. But, you know, I'm an adult—I drink coffee and stuff—even I can show a little grace every now and then. And that's what I did. I waited quietly in the hallway with my sister, then quietly near the soda machines with a Hispanic guy in red Rangers sweatpants with tubes up his nostrils, not so quietly in the men's room, and then quietly again with my sister. And when AJ finally came out I was the first to squeeze his shoulders and shake my head and say things like, "Rough, huh?" and "This is so hard," and "Anyway . . ."

"She doesn't want to talk to you right now," my brother said.

"Yeah," I said. "Right."

"Seriously. She said she's too tired."

"Well when does she wanna talk to me?"

"I don't know man—like, maybe tomorrow?"

I thought he might be kidding, but after some aggressive back-and-forth about it I came to terms with the fact.

My mother remained too tired to speak to me for the next several days, and for the most part I think I handled it in an understanding, patient, and mature style, except for one incident down at The Wharf when I punched some guy's hamburger.

On day three, my mother felt up to talking with me.

"Please don't cry or we won't get through this," she said. "Please. Let's just say what we need to say to each other. OK?"

"OK," I said, crying.

"OK," she said.

"Should I go first?"

She closed her eyes and nodded.

"OK," I said. "What exactly are we supposed to say here?"

"Whatever you feel you need to."

"OK," I said. "Well, I mean, it's not a big deal or anything but, it doesn't really make sense that you picked AJ to come in here before me. I mean, I was the middle child and he was the last and a C-section so . . . and then I had to wait so long and I got nervous about it, I thought maybe we'd never get to talk and I punched a paper-towel dispenser and some guy in the dinner and—Are you still awake?"

"Yes," she said. But her eyes stayed closed.

"Well?"

"I don't know why," she said. "Is there anything else you want to say to me?"

"I love you?" Then I started sobbing.

"That it?" she asked.

"Yeah," I said. "That's it."

She pinched the bed sheet between her thumb and index finger, then dropped it. "So you have no complaints about me as a mother or anything?"

"No," I said. "You've been a great mom. I couldn't ask for anything more. I had a great childhood."

She nodded and squeezed my hand. "OK then," she said. "Well, I have something I'd like to say to you."

"All right," I said. "What is it?"

"One time you threw a book at me. You were home from college, and you were really angry with me about something, and you threw a book at my head."

I had no recollection of this at all. I wondered if it was the painkillers talking again.

"Did it hit you?" I asked.

"No. I ducked and it hit the wall."

"Wow," I said. "I really don't remember that." We blinked at each other. "Honestly," I said, shaking my head. "I don't."

"Well I do," she said. "And I'm telling you because I don't want you to ever, *ever*, be abusive with a woman again. You can't abuse women, Alby. I need you to promise me that."

"OK," I said. "I promise."

"You promise what?"

"I promise I won't abuse ladies."

"Ever," she said.

"Ever," I said. "I won't abuse ladies *ever*."

"OK," she said, rubbing my hand a little, giving it a pat and a squeeze. Then she said she was tired and asked me to leave. I stood up and kissed her on the forehead and walked to the door.

"I really don't remember that."

"I believe you," she said. "Now shut off the lights, please."

"OK," I said, and flipped the switch.

Immediately after closing the door I rushed over to my brother and sister and told them everything, then asked if they remembered hearing about it. My sister said no, but that it sounded like something I'd do, and I told her to shut the fuck up.

My brother said he kinda did remember something like that, that he thinks maybe he remembers her telling him about it over the phone one day. I pressed him for details, then and on numerous occasions since, but the only other thing he's said about it—years later over beers and a bottle of bourbon, after I got real pushy—was that it made sense because I was at the peak of my asshole stage back then. Then he paused and looked off and added, "The first peak."

She died not long after, and after years of racking my brain over it I eventually came to some vague remembrance of the incident. Nothing concrete, just sitting at the kitchen table, a book in front of me, her standing there, the both of us yelling. That's all. Of course that could be from any number of times we yelled at each other in the kitchen, or it could be complete invention, something I dreamed up in response to all this. Either way, though, I believe it. I believe I threw that book. I must have.

And now here my sister was using it against me, because she thought, correctly, that it would hurt. The best I could think to come back at her with was "Learn about dishwashers, retard." She smirked and shook her head. "Also," I added, "stop cutting the split ends off your dykey hairdo and leaving them on the sink 'cause it's fuckin' disgusting, and so is your dandruff. You should try T/Gel 'cause apple cider vinegar isn't doing the job, you fuckin' hippie asshole. And stop throwing your bloody toilet paper from your gross shaved legs in the bathroom garbage cause fuckin' Sparkles fuckin' smells the blood and then fuckin' knocks over the garbage can and fuckin' eats it. OK? And nobody wants to go to the bathroom and see bloody fuckin' toilet paper in the fuckin' garbage. So fuck you."

She name-called me some more, so I mocked her in my mocking voice. I went: "This is you: *I'm too busy doing important artwork to be considerate of other people and clean up after myself so instead I'm gonna cover every flat surface with my shit so other people can't eat at the table without moving my shit around. Also, I'm a dumb cunt.* That's you, you dumb cunt."

With that she began shoving me through the doorway yelling, "Get out! Get out! Get the fuck out!" And I'm not kidding
when I say she's super strong and almost had me out, and I
wasn't putting up much of a fight at all, was almost willingly
going, and then I just thought: No, *you* get out. As she shoved
me again I grabbed her shirt, and honestly it was a case of being
stronger than I think I am, because she kinda went flying
through the air and landed on the ground on her back. We
were both shocked, me probably more so. She got up quick
though and charged, dealing punches left and right (add that
to the list: #8—she hit me first), which didn't accomplish much
except to back me up a few feet into the kitchen. Eventually
she stopped to survey the damage, and I grinned at her. She
charged again, swinging wildly, and I blocked what I could,
then shoved her off. When she came at me a third time I threw
one medium-powered punch at the middle of her chest that
kinda skimmed over the right tit and landed solidly on the left,
sending her backward over the dishwasher door, which was
still open with plenty of space available for pots and pans. There
were, however, a few utensils in the utensil holder thing, including a knife with I think cream cheese on it that she grabbed on
the way up. I turned and ran. I'd just made it outside when I
heard it bang off the back of the back door.

We avoided each other for the rest of the night and most of
the following day, until our father came home from work
jacked up on Ritalin, acting like a dick, the specifics of which
I don't recall and which don't matter. What does matter is that
shared suffering can lead to a sense of solidarity—false maybe,
temporary for sure—so we ganged up on him till he fled up

the stairs to his room to play Sudoku or some shit on his computer. My sister and I spent the next few hours at the kitchen table guzzling whatever alcohol was left in the house, pledging allegiance to each other, promising it wouldn't happen again, that we're sorry, we're sorry. We're so sorry.

LITTLE THINGS

I folded my arms. They felt big, capable of anything. Lifting, carrying, digging, feeding cows PCP so they revolt with unexpected and tremendous violence—anything. Wrapping gifts in tissue paper and busting teeth out of Christian heads, painting things pink and planting weeds because they're treated unfairly. Pumping bicycle tires, pumping gas, pumping iron, bagging my own groceries and skipping boulders across the Long Island Sound all the way to Connecticut. Cracking eggs with one hand and folding laundry. Pushing my Mexican neighbor's broke-down car across the street Thursday mornings to avoid street sweeping tickets and tossing my cell phone to a friend who needs to make an important call to his mom. Opening every jar for every lady. Helping. I felt like helping. I felt like I could help.

———

The first thing I did was clean the microwave. I went from there. Sometimes I succeeded, sometimes there were other times. I've witnessed people break, cry, collapse, kill themselves, get killed, or get old. I've seen people lose their hair, their minds, their driver's licenses. My father lost his gallbladder after dieting with Nutri-system. What could I do? I mopped the kitchen floor, took a walk, saw a dead baby rabbit with a bicycle tire tread through its middle. It reminded me of a friend of mine named Nicky who had hairy legs and liked fireworks. One summer he caught his girlfriend cheating, sprinted from her doorstep toward Vanderbilt Boulevard and dove in front of a station wagon with a couple of kids in the backseat.

I saw an old lady in 7-Eleven wearing a nightgown, with red mittens on her feet and blue veins in her ankles. I bought potato chips. People got married. They got houses and they got furniture and they trusted the government and they got fat. There was a homeless man with long hair, a black leather jacket, green cutoff shorts, and a mental problem that he tried to walk off like a Little League baseball injury. Walking, walking, always walking. He was very tan. The locals called him "the man with a million miles on his feet." The police shot him in the back when he didn't stop to answer their questions.

I remember sitting in the passenger seat of my father's diesel after a Roy Rogers dinner. My brother was in the back. A car a couple of cars in front of us swerved left, then the next car swerved, then the next, until the car directly in front us didn't swerve. We watched in the headlights as three puppies rolled out from underneath it, leaned closer to them as my father braked, steered around and past and pulled over. On the side of the road two of them looked just fine except they were dead. The third was bleeding, it was hard to tell from where exactly, there was a lot of blood, but it kept breathing for a few minutes before it stopped and died in the on-and-off orange of my father's hazards.

People ate veal. I dated a chubby Catholic girl who told me her parents never touched her, that as a kid she wanted to be touched so badly she looked forward to the lice and scoliosis tests at school. I knew a guy in junior high who told everyone he owned a baby elephant; years later he murdered his step-mother by beating her head in with a can of Chicken & Stars soup. I saw cats, dogs, possums, raccoons and squirrels, a fox, a kangaroo, a bear, deer, rabbits and birds, toads, rats and mice and snakes with their guts smashed out, their insides out-side, their heads crushed and dead on sunny roadsides. My mother had cancer.

I came home, held her hand, pushed her pain button, did her nails and fluffed her pillows, brushed her teeth and emp-tied her piss bag. I bought her stuffed animals and licorice and long straws so she could drink her juice in bed. She mostly just slept and vomited. Her hospital room was noisy. There was lots of moaning, beds creaking, PCA pumps beeping, nurses com-ing and going and laughing and asking, How are you on a scale of zero to ten, zero being no pain and ten being the worst pain you've ever felt? Twelve.

Three months into it my brother and I were watching the Dilaudid drip, listening to her mumble "ow ow ow" in her sleep, when her eyes opened wide, then wider, then came back together in a real slow drug-drunk blink. Then she threw her sheet on the floor, picked her hospital gown up over her head. "No more fucking water."

I said, "Do you want me to go to the Coke machine?"

"Why are you trying to kill me?"

"We're not."

"Do you realize I'm laying here, full frontal?"

"Yes."

"Are you happy to see your mother full frontal?"

"Not really."

"Then get out."

We sat there unsure of what to do or say, where to look. She yelled there was salt on her legs, something about conductors and the procedure and don't touch my antique fork. She ripped the IVs out of her arms, the Hickman port out of her chest. Blood shot up in the air. I grabbed her as my brother went running down the hall toward the nurses' station, screaming. I held her down by the wrists—it wasn't difficult, she hadn't been eating, maybe weighed eighty-five pounds at that point. When she was through struggling she just kinda collapsed in on herself and cried. I said, "Mom," like it was a question.

Later, after they had strapped her to the bed, bandaged her up, shot her full of strong whatever until she passed out, redid her IVs in her feet so she couldn't reach them, after we had called our father and lied that everything was fine and he should take the night off, called our sister and told her what happened, then regretted it, we smoked a couple of cigarettes out front with a transporter who had burned his hand with cinnamon-roll icing and decided we'd both spend the night. Back in the room, after we sat there watching the Dilaudid drip, not speaking for half an hour, just listening to our mother mumble "ow ow ow" in her sleep, I turned to my brother and said, "Yo, her vagina's in a lot better shape than I thought it'd be."

He considered it for a second, then nodded in agreement.

She came home to die. Hospice delivered a bed, equipment, boxes of meds, and a lady doctor who told us one to three days. We set her up in the den, under the ceiling fan my sister had tied little glass dragonflies to with string. My mother seemed to like watching them fly their circle around the room but I didn't. I got good at spackling, got impressed with bubble gum's resistance to decay, ate her Ativan like aspirin. I told her that I'd miss her, that I hated her body for getting sick, that I wanted to seize god or fate or the universe by the throat and make it leave her alone. She laughed at me. Her bedsores leaked an awful-smelling fluid. My brother, sister, and I took turns changing her bandages and sheets, drank her liquid Valium, and played UNO. We watched our father watch her dying, learned from the grief on his face every time he walked in the room. He never lasted more than ten minutes. A priest came to give her last rites and I gave him my meanest look. He asked me if I'd like to receive Communion and I gave him a different mean-est look and walked out of the room. A week later the lady doctor came back, said one to three days again. My brother and I wrote each other cheerer-upper notes on brown napkins:

Do you worry that Mom will see your gay thoughts from heaven?

No. Do you worry she gets X-ray vision and sees the unde-scended testicles in your girlfriend's abdomen?

That girlfriend, Tara, came over later that day and hung around like she was part of the family, then cooked us a chicken for dinner. Just as we sat down to eat it my brother said I should do the dishes. I said, "You're kidding?" He said he wasn't. I told him that I wasn't gonna do any damn dishes until he cleaned his IBS shit shrapnel off the fuckin' toilet. His face turned red. I said, "Looks like you might wanna hit me. If you do I'm going to stab you in the head with my fork." Then I took a bite of the chicken—it was pretty good—and he punched it out of my mouth; cracked me right in the jaw. I was so shocked that I didn't do anything for two whole seconds and neither did anyone else. Then I lunged at him, strangled him, smashed his head into the kitchen counter. He started bleeding from somewhere in his hair, his girlfriend started pulling mine, and my sister wedged herself in between us. I think she caught a stray or two before we all fell into the empty beer bottles on top of the radiator. My father came wobble-running in like a gorilla, yelling something I couldn't quite understand because Tara was clawing at my ears.

Outside in the driveway I caught my breath, smoked a cigarette, stomped on a disk of ice frozen into the upside-down lid of a green garbage can, shook. A few minutes later my sister came out with my jacket and asked if I was all right. I said I was and asked if my brother was all right. She said he had a pretty good cut on his head but seemed all right. For the first time in a long time I felt relief, like I had just fucked or cried or quit a job. It feels good to be punched in the face, to punch someone in the face. I walked over to the dock and stared at the boats for a while, then headed to the Mexican restaurant around the corner and drank Budweiser. Twenty minutes later my father showed up, said he followed my footprints in the snow. I asked him if he wanted to do a shot of something, anything. He said, "If I start drinkin' now I won't stop." Just then my brother called my phone.

He said, "Hey man."

I said, "Hey man."

"Did you really stab me?"

"No."

"Are you gonna do the dishes?"

"Yeah, I'll do the dishes."

"Cool."

"Is Mom still alive?"

"Yeah."

"Cool."

She died a week later. I got a job gutting houses.

I worked with an interesting guy who smoked things off tinfoil; he'd had a rough childhood and adulthood's rough on everyone. We were ripping vinyl tiles out of a kitchen when he told me that a twenty-eight-year-old girl he knew was working at Lord & Taylor when her heart exploded. He told me just like that, plain, not angry at all. I told him that a fifteen-year-old from Bayport stepped in front of an LIRR train and let it run her down.

"I heard about that," he said. "Dragged her body a mile."

Also, two bicyclists were killed by one car on Sunrise Highway and a twenty-year-old died of a drug overdose a block from our house. Her daughter was three. Every year someone drowns in Lake Ronkonkoma and thousands of toads drown in swimming pools. A good friend's kid brother got killed in Iraq, a really pretty girl I met in San Francisco went to sleep one night and didn't wake up, and a guy I know didn't have health insurance when he was diagnosed with multiple sclerosis.

The restaurant he worked at was kind enough to have a fund-raiser for him that grossed over eight thousand dollars. They gave him six hundred.

A few weeks later I went to lunch with my family, asked my sister how she was doing since Mom. She just looked at me and let her eyes water. I asked my dad the same question. He just pointed to my sister like, I feel like that. My brother shrugged. I told them that I was OK, which might've been true, that I'd help them if I knew how. The waitress came over, dressed in all black including the apron, called me "Ma'am, sir . . . ma'am." I said, "Do I look like a lady to you?" She stammered an apology, said she hadn't looked closely enough, which was strange because she was avoiding looking at me while she spoke. I didn't eat much, just picked at my french fries and drank ice water while they ate and argued about the will, about the money. I didn't know what I thought about the money except that I didn't feel like arguing about it. We're not a dessert family but we like black coffee. I was almost done with my cup when my sister said she went to the cemetery and ate some of the grass off our mother's grave. My father reached for his wallet.

When we got home there was a baby bird in the driveway, lying there, featherless. It was tiny. Its skin was almost see-through. We were all just standing around it—looking. I said, "I'll go get something to put it in," and started toward the house. My father said maybe the best thing to do would be to back over it with the car.

IF P, THEN Q

In the middle of solving an equation on the board my eleventh-grade calculus teacher, Mr. McGar, dropped the chalk, which broke into pieces on the floor. He looked down at the pieces for a few seconds, then turned to the class, and said, "As a kid I used to catch bumblebees in a butterfly net. When I caught one I'd put it in an upside-down jar, then I'd slide a tissue soaked in alcohol underneath the rim of the jar, which would knock the bee unconscious. I would then very carefully tie a string around the bumblebee's neck, and after a few minutes the bumblebee would wake up, and I would have him on a leash." Then he walked over to the window and stared out past the parking lot filled with cars that looked alike.

So I studied math as an undergrad until I tried, using modus tollens, to prove to Kate Damon that she should date me. It didn't work, and I realized that math would not get me what I wanted, so I dropped out and started drinking a lot of well whiskey in a bar around the corner from the apartment I would eventually be evicted from. Money ran out quickly, and more out of boredom than habit, I kept going to the ATM checking to see if a balance would somehow appear in my account. It never did, and so I learned a little green Spanish and spent hours doing finger puppetry for the ATM camera. I got pretty good at it.

I can do a dog, a rabbit, a lizard, an elephant, a hawk, and an eagle (there's a difference in the thumbs). I can do a donkey, a squirrel, a cow, a cobra, a horse, and a pig. I also do a mouse and make him say *ee ee ee* and then I also do myself and he says, "What? I can't hear you, Ma."

Mom, my left hand, asks, "What's wrong, Alby?"

My right hand goes, "It's the little things, the little things, Ma. They're relentless."

"Why are you so angry?"

"I don't know, Ma. I don't know."

Excuse me, a voice behind me said. *I need to use the ATM.*

I didn't say anything, just stuffed my hands in my pants pockets and walked off thinking about what to do next.

Rape in the
Animal Kingdom

What I did was mix a cup of cat food with a quarter-cup of applesauce, a TUMS smooth dissolve tablet ground to powder, a hard-boiled egg and water until it was the approximate consistency of cooked oatmeal. I did that because that's what it said to do online. It also said online to cut the end of a straw to make a small scoop, to feed it every fourteen to twenty minutes from sunrise to sunset, that you should never put liquids directly into its mouth or it could drown, to keep it warm, and that despite your best efforts 90 to 95 percent will die, good luck. With luck like that, I didn't name him at first. I didn't think I could stand losing another thing with a name. When he lasted a week, I called him Gary.

Gary was, for the most part, at least to start off with, almost transparent. He looked like a dog's heart with a bird's head stuck on, a blob with a beak, and one time when I was leaning in real close to better see the veins pumping blood under his skin he woke up and bit me on the nose and started chirping like crazy. I shushed him and fed him till he stopped chirping like crazy and closed his eyes and went back to sleep. Then I just watched him breathe for a while, making sure he wasn't dead.

One morning when I was making sure he wasn't dead there was a knock on my bedroom door and my father popped his toupee-ed head in.

"Made you breakfast," he said. "Steak and eggs."

"We don't have steak," I said. "Or eggs. So I know you're lying."

"I did," he insisted, but really he didn't because what he'd actually made me was a chicken-and-cheese Hot Pocket that he thought was a steak-and-egg Hot Pocket, because for some reason he'd thrown out the boxes and Hot Pockets all look the same. None of that matters. What matters is that when my losing-his-mind father saw Gary's setup on my desk, he told me I was losing mine.

Maybe I was. By this point I'd abandoned the laundry-lint-in-cereal-bowl nest because the lint was getting stuck in Gary's pinfeathers, instead opting for crumpled hand towels in a small Easter basket suspended with string from the handle of a large Easter basket. For decor and scent's sake I'd paper-clamped on some pinecones and twigs, then fastened a large oak leaf over the whole thing to shade him from the lamp. Finally, I bought a big wooden G from the local arts and crafts store and painted it the same green as a horsefly eye, then glued it to the handle of the big basket.

"What are you," my father asked me, the sun coming through the window, lighting half his face, "crazy now?"

If I could go back I'd answer differently. I'd lie that I was fine, or make a joke, or tell him the truth: that I was just trying to get through it. That I was having a hard time. That—and I know how hollow and sentimental this sounds, how lame—I missed my mother in a way that felt anaerobic. I couldn't get my air back; at one point I literally stuck my head out the car window and opened my mouth to force it in.

"What do you mean *now*?" I said.

It fell flat in front of us, like a stupid fact, and there was nothing left for him to do but hobble over to get a better look. After he got it he turned to better-look at me, and then he better-looked at Gary's setup again.

"Listen," I said, "he's helpless and he needs me, and I got a thing in my heart for helpless things that need me, OK? So I'm gonna be here for him until he dies or grows into a god-damned falcon that flies around the neighborhood all day eating raccoons and dogs and little toddlers before he flies back to my forearm and takes shits. I already ordered the glove, dude—online—'cause Gary here is gonna terrorize all of Suffolk County, hunting mammals and butt-fucking seagulls."

"Why you gotta talk like that?" he said. "You sound stupid."

"Yeah," I said, "people keep telling me that, but people also keep being pieces a shit that are wrong. So let me tell you something else that'll sound stupid: right now, Gary's stem cells are generating rods and cones for better night vision that he'll use to bite people's dicks off in the dark. Dudes' dicks are in danger, Dad. And if you don't think so, you can get right the fuck out of my bedroom!"

He said "Calm down" like he meant it, then "Sure they are" like he didn't, then "How's he doing?" like he did again.

"Great," I said. "He can already pick his head up like it's nothing. Watch."

The two of us scooched closer to the Easter baskets and I scooped some food-mush onto the straw and stuck it near his bird-face. "Demo time, bro. Hup-hup. Eat this for strength!" But Gary didn't move at all, not even when I tapped his beak with it.

"You sure he's alive?" my father asked.

"Yeah I'm sure he's alive," I said, offended and straw-pointing. "If you look right here you can see he's breathing. He's probably just dreaming of things to rape. He's a freak, this one. A real pervert."

"Christ," my father said. And with that he headed for the door, then stopped and without turning around added, "Come down when you're hungry."

"I'm hungry right now," I said. "For breakfast and revenge."

He shook his head and said one word—"Stupid"—then ducked out and lumbered down the stairs, his hand sliding along the iron railing a beat behind each footfall—step, slide, step, slide—which I only knew because I could hear it. I made sure Gary was still breathing again before putting a clean washcloth over him and tucking him in, then joined my father in the kitchen, where we huddled holding lukewarm Hot Pockets over paper towels, not speaking to each other. I can't say about his, but my head was filled with birds. Hawky ones. Killers.

Even though I had no way of knowing exactly how old Gary was when we found him, I convinced myself that his feathers had started coming in three days ahead of schedule. I was as idiotically proud as all those bragging parents I despise when Baby learns to flip itself over or eat bananas or whatever. Anything he did—and some things he didn't—I took as a sign of progress. How much he ate or didn't, slept or didn't, chirped or didn't were all reason for celebration and praise. So the sight of him popping his head up over the wicker of his basket and looking around the desk one white-bright morning filled me with such joy I leapt out of bed, knocking over a stool. Yes! I thought, fists pumping. *Yes!!!* "Let me give you the tour, bro," I said to him. "That's my fuckin' stapler right there, vintage, and those are some pencils in a jar. But you don't even need to worry about that. You only need to worry about three things: how to fly, how to hunt, and how to fuck." I clapped and pointed at him. "Also how to communicate with your birdie friends and bite dudes' dicks off in the dark, so that's five things. Better get to work." And that's when I started playing him YouTube videos of eagles throwing goats off cliffs and falcons swooping down to eat snakes. One morning I was showing him a clip of a dolphin with a boner raping a snorkeler, and Gary cocked his head at it, hopped out of his basket-nest onto the desk, and shit next to my bottle of wood glue.

"Pay attention," I said. "This is important."

Around eleven my sister called through the door that I'd received a package. I told her to come in. "It's probably a dowry from some girls that want to get pregnant by me. I read somewhere that putting egg whites up pussies helps sperm swim—works like a luge."

She craned her head to read the return address. "No, it's from falcon gloves dot com."

"Even better," I said, taking it from her. "Now get the hell outta here. Gary and I have a lot of training to do today."

"What kind of training?"

"Well," I said, "Gary's going through puberty right now, and it won't be long before he's enjoying the fruits of adulthood: flying around, eating berries, making Asian people wear surgical masks—you know. We're just finishing up our morning video tutorials, and then we're going on a field trip to the front lawn. Gary here needs to learn to take care of himself in the wild, so I'm gonna let him hop around the grass for a while."

She poked Gary's basket with her index finger so it swung like a cradle. "That's it?"

"No. I might put him on a tree branch, too. I don't know yet."

"Cool," she said, poking his basket again. "I wanna help."

I looked at her face trying to gauge her sincerity but got distracted by the tiny blond hairs running the length of her jaw.

"Fine. But if you interfere, you're banned forever."

I don't even know why I said it. Banning each other forever was supposed to mean something but didn't, at least not to her. When I was about ten and she was thirteen, she'd tell me jokes after dinner to make me laugh so hard I'd throw up. It was a trick she discovered by accident one night, as my giggling turned into an airless, wheezing laugh, followed by a cough, followed by chewed-up chicken nuggets on the floor.

But once she realized the trick could be repeated, she did it so often I started losing weight. It'd been going on for a few weeks, and she'd already been told to quit, already been made to promise to quit, and already been grounded, but each stopped her only long enough for our parents to let their guard down. I was in the top bunk with the lights off already when I heard *"Pssst. Pssssssssssst. Psst!"* I knew what was about to happen and started giggling, my brother in the bottom bunk below me whisper-pleading for her to stop. "It's not a joke," she whispered. "I just need to ask you an important question."

"What," I said.

"Why'd the monkey fall out of the tree?"

"Get outta here!" AJ yelled, and that was enough, and my body did its wheeze and cough thing before a plate's worth of Hamburger Helper went waterfalling down over the railing while our brother huddled in the back corner of his bed crying for help. My mother came running in with a bottle of Windex and rags and screamed at my sister that she was banned forever from telling me jokes after dinner. She delivered the punchline three nights later on her way past the door.

"Because it was dead," she said. Spaghetti.

And that day on the lawn, with Gary, was like that. We were adults now, but still the laughing came easy. Dad went for sandwiches and sodas at the deli and the three of us sat in the sun watching Gary hop around the grass like a toad between us. We were splayed out, switching from our hands to our elbows and back again, ripping up lawn and tossing it while we told old stories and laughed, I mean really laughed, for the first time in months. My face hurt. I was in the middle of telling them what I discovered about hooligan penguins gay gangbanging each other when AJ drove in for a long week-end, and then we were all sitting there having a good time together near tulip buds bursting purple. I pointed out their yellow stamens and said "flower dicks" while Gary bounced around like an idiot-machine. AJ couldn't believe he was still alive.

"What kind of bird is he, you think?" he asked.

"A dragon," I said. "Or some kind of raptor."

"Sparrow," my dad said.

"Osprey maybe," I said. "Murderer of fish."

"Yeah, he looks like a sparrow," my brother said.

"He does look like a sparrow," my sister said.

"And you guys look like dumb-shits that don't know what they're talking about," I said, "because sparrows are the Toyota Camrys of birds: every car looks like them and they look like every car and sometimes even minivans."

"That doesn't make sense," my brother said.

"Yeah it does. Ford Taurus. Honda Accord. Mercedes Benz . . . I can't tell the difference."

"He has Mom's pills hidden in his room," my sister said.

"They're my inheritance," I said. "She bequeathed them to me when you guys weren't there, but the point I'm trying to make here is that things often look like other things that they're not. It's too early to tell what Gary is, and it doesn't even matter because he's imprinted on me. I am his guardian, confidant, and mentor—"

"You're a gay," my father said.

"—and the example I'm setting for him is that of alpha-male penguin-swan-hawk. If I do my job correctly, he'll be capable of amazing sexual and regular-style violence on land, sea, air, ice, and telephone pole power lines. I'm talking trans- gressive *and* cute. Identify and swoop. Seek and destroy. Right, Gary?"

And at that exact moment little Gary hopped up onto my knee and moved his head around weirdly, kinda like an Egyp- tian, and sing-songed something like, "Purty, purty, purty . . . whoit, whoit, whoit, whoit . . . what-cheer, what-cheer . . . wheet, wheet, wheet, wheet!"

All of us oohed and aahed.

It was another week before Gary figured out how to fly into walls, and then his aim improved and he figured out how to fly into my face. "Watch the talons," I'd say. He tried to land on Sparkles's face a few times, too, but she'd get scared and run out of the room. It was amusing to me—an obese bulldog getting spooked by a bird no bigger than a tangerine. But after like the fourth or fifth time I wanted them to be friends, just in case, so I called Sparkles back in and held Gary up for her inspection. She sniffed him for a few seconds, looked at me, sniffed him some more, then licked him. On top of the pills, I was drinking every night because my heart felt like how hearts feel when you lose someone you love forever, but when Spar- kles did that my heart hurt a whole different way that I can't explain except to say it felt like a broken tooth—the gesture was too sweet, and it sent a jangly, electric pain shooting through me. "Shit," I said, wiping my eyes. "Goddammit." Then I made whimpering noises like my mother had near the end. I petted Sparkles and put Gary in his basket and bolted out of my room and down the stairs and out the front door and down the steps and across the lawn, where I dove into the shrubs bordering the property and just lay in them facedown for a while, until my father came outside and found me there and asked if I was OK. "I'm freakin' worried," he said. "What're you doin'?"

"Nothing. I just—I had to be in this bush for a couple minutes. Now I feel better."

"Well how long you gonna stay there? I heard Gary chirpin'. I could feed him if you want."

"Oh," I said. "No. That's OK. Just help me outta here."

Without another word—and I appreciated that—my father grabbed my ankles and yanked hard, twice, until I was out and lying facedown on the lawn. I push-upped my way to standing and thanked him, then slapped him on his big belly and ran into the house and up the stairs to feed my bird who, when he saw me come in, extended his neck like a turtle and opened his mouth as wide as he could and chirped like crazy. I was about to feed him when my father ducked in and said, "I wanna do it."

I looked at him standing there in the doorway, doubledenimed, his hat literally in his hand. His eyes were bloodshot and the same washed-out blue as a brand of dish soap I buy.

"OK," I said. "Sure."

He walked over and I handed him the straw and gave him instructions: "Scoop some mush on there and put it near his face." He did, and Gary chomped at it, and then again and again, until he'd had his fill and shut up and went back to sleep, and then we leaned in and watched him breathe, making sure

he wasn't dead. After a while, more to himself than me, my
father said, "Cool."

I was eating breakfast when my sister marched in and slapped
down a photograph of a bird that wasn't just similar to Gary,
it was near exact: the grayish-brown coloring with a slight
reddish tint on the wings and tail feathers; the raised crest and
coral-colored cone-shaped beak; the poofy underparts and per-
verted look in the eyes. Underneath the photo: NORTHERN
CARDINAL, FEMALE.

I didn't even finish my Hot Pocket.

On my way up the stairs I was considering a name change,
but decided against it because I thought it might be bad luck
to change names, like with a boat, and anyway Gary thought
I was his mom so whatever. When I got to my room I found
him hanging out under my bed near a balled-up sock that I'd
thought was lost forever.

"Why are you always on the ground?" I said. "It's a good
way to get eaten, dipshit. Plus you're gonna hurt yourself flying around the room banging into walls like a racquetball. Guess
it's time I built you that aviary. But first, research."

I stuck my hand out and Gary jumped into it. I placed him
on the top edge of my laptop screen, then read everything I
could find, twice. Taxonomy: *Cardinalis cardinalis*; common
name, Northern Cardinal; native to southern Canada, the east
coasts of North America down through Mexico, Guatemala,
and Belize, and vagrant in the Cayman Islands, which seems like
a smart place to be a vagrant even though topless sunbathing

is prohibited by law. Most often they live at the edges of woods, thickets, fields, and marshes and are ground feeders that enjoy eating dumbass insects as well as wild fruits, berries, oats, and seeds. They also drink maple sap from holes made by sapsuckers, an example of commensalism—look it up. Northern cardinals don't migrate and don't molt into an ugly plumage, so they're still good-looking motherfuckers in the snow. Their predators include owls and hawks, snakes, raccoons and squirrels, red foxes, dickheaded brats with BB guns, and kinda-sorta cowbirds, the deadbeat parents of the avian world, who lay their eggs in the cuplike nests of cardinals and never come back. Northern cardinals mate for life and don't rape anything. On the plus side, males are extremely aggressive in defending their territory, so much so that they often attack their own reflections in windows and break their little red necks. They're so cool and great that they're the official bird of seven U.S. states I won't name. Also, young birds, both male and female, show coloring similar to the adult female until the fall, when males molt and grow their super-looking adult feathers.

I plucked Gary off my laptop, stared him right in his left eyeball, then flipped him over but didn't see anything. So I put him down on the desk and did a search for bird dicks and discovered that there are only a few species of birds with actual dicks, and even those are retractable. I can't say about the ostriches, emus, cassowaries, or kiwis, but ducks and other waterfowl sometimes fuck in the water or go swimming right after, and having a dick helps ensure that the sperm isn't washed away. Their cocks are corkscrew-shaped, and lady ducks have the plumbing to match. Their sex is referred to as coercive,

which means rapey, which is exactly the kind of sex this elephant has with this rhino in a video Gary and I watched about
a hundred times. That and the one where the donkey with a
purple boner knocks over a South American guy shitting in a
field. It's pretty good.

I built the aviary out on the covered porch with mosquito netting my mother had rigged up around her bed for no reason,
hex-head concrete anchors, and the biggest stones I could find.
When that was all in place, my father and I took a trip to a
birding store out in Sayville, where I bought two houses and
three perches that I mounted to the stucco at different heights,
about seven feet and four feet. Then I dragged the potted Ficus
out there and plopped it right in the middle so Gary could
learn to hang out in trees. It was a concern of mine, and I
wouldn't let him outside until he learned to get off the ground
more and could feed himself. I didn't sleep well the first few
nights because I was worried he might be lonely or worse, and
on the fourth night I dragged my sleeping bag and pillow out
there and curled up on the cool concrete next to his basket. He
woke me at dawn by crash-landing into my face.

And that's how it stayed for a week or so. Things kind of
plateaued. Gary wouldn't feed himself, wouldn't stay in the
birdhouse or on the perches or in the tree. He just hopped
around the concrete all day making his little metallic chips and
chirps, waiting for one of us to feed him. I didn't know what to
do but give him time and space, let him build up some self-
reliance. I was feeling cooped-up and spring-feverish anyway,
having spent six months dealing with my mother's diagnosis,

five watching her die, two since she up and did. It felt—if not good—better to be outside, and the girls were wearing less and less the warmer it got. At one point I was buying coffee in 7-Eleven and sprung a halfie looking at the woman-next-to-me's newly pink shoulder, the few freckles, the white of her bra strap. Her hair smelled like the concrete at a car wash. It took all of my restraint not to press my index finger against her shoulder burn and watch it go from white to pink.

I started going for long jogs, dinner with friends, drinks after. Between my sister and father someone was usually around, and both were more than happy to check in on Gary, make sure he was all right. He always was, even when Jackie and I took him out to the backyard to shoot video of him flying over to me and landing on my falcon glove. The plan was to dub in audio of a Crested Eagle shriek, maybe an Andean Condor. We did three takes, all failures. The first one he flew into my chest and fell to the ground, the second into my hairdo, and the third time he went over my head and up onto a pine tree branch about twenty feet off the ground. He wouldn't come down, and I had to get a ladder and crab net and scoop him. And that's when I enacted the Tether Rule: Gary wasn't allowed outside without a kite string tied to his leg. My sister started calling him Tampon.

Later that week I ran into a drunken ex at The Wharf, and when the opportunity presented itself, I took her by the hand to the parking lot and my car, where we leaned against the hood and French and freestyle kissed for a few minutes before climbing in. We fooled around until someone's headlights head-lighted us up and she told me to stop what I was doing, which was fingering her C'mere style—like, *You're in big trouble now, Vagina. Get over here this instant!* When I didn't stop she said stop again, and I was like, "Really?" and she was like, "Yes really," and I was like, "No," and she was like, "Stop," and I was like, "Please?" and she was like, "STOP!" and I was like, "*Fine.*" Then I stopped. She took her heel out of the cup holder and a penny was stuck to it.

After a quick discussion we decided to go to her place where I got her naked and fingered her Vending Machine style, like I'm trying to get change out of a vending machine—before attempting the Switcheroo, this move I do where I switch my fingers with my boner real fast and hope she doesn't notice, but she noticed, and since I didn't have a condom on, since I didn't have a condom with me, she slapped me right on the dick and I watched it waggle like a windshield wiper. I went back to C'mere-ing her just long enough for her to start enjoying it, then Shoehorned her—a maneuver where instead of switching I go up and under and "shoehorn" it in—and it totally worked and we unprotecto-ed for ten to fifteen before I came in her light brown pubes and belly button and fell asleep for not very long because I woke up to a call from my father at six. Even in that blurry state, I knew before I answered. "I'll come home" is all I said, and hung up.

When I got there he pointed to a space in the mosquito netting. "I heard Sparkles barkin' around five," he said. "Some chirpin', too. But by the time I got down the stairs he was gone. Musta been a stray cat or raccoon or somethin'."

"Maybe he got out," I said. "Maybe he got away."

"I don't think so, kid."

"Well you don't have to think so. You just gotta help me look."

So we looked, scouring the ground and the shrubs and the trees around the house, calling out for him. Whistling, like we were happy.

That afternoon I didn't get drunk. I went to the mall for some reason, where I ran my hands along the clothes hanging in department stores and rode the escalators, cleaning my shoes on the bristles, giving people dirty looks. I ended up in the food court and bought a fountain soda, pushed down the little plastic bubble things on the lid—COLA, DIET, RB, OTHER— took a few sips, and threw it in an overfilled garbage can on my way into this specialty grocery store. I wandered around there for a while, then stood poking packages of meat, thinking all kinds of things. Like I couldn't make him mean enough. Belligerent enough. The-right-combination-of-fearless-and-fearful enough. Like I failed him. Like I should have been there. Like I'm a cowbird. A man dressed in blood-flecked all-white asked if he could help me.

"No," I said. "You can't."

Then I got drunk. I was sitting in the back room of The Wharf watching the raindrops race down the windows in stop-and-go jig-jags. I looked through them at the Great South Bay, the drops doing their concentric-circle thing on the blue-brown surface of the water as two mute swans swam by. Mute swans are an invasive species in North America and an altogether nasty, ill-tempered dickhead of a bird. Often they're used as "watchdogs" to keep geese and other

waterfowl out of private ponds. Their aggression isn't lim-
ited to the water, either. On land it's not uncommon for them
to spread their wings and chase people down footpaths or
across lawns. They hiss and bark. They've even killed people,
kind of, knocking them out of canoes and kayaks and pecking
them on the head until they drown. Growing up I used to hate
them, but I understand now. It works. Mute swans are thriving.

    I finished my drink and headed to the darkest part of the
parking lot and punched a car window until my hand busted
and the window didn't. Then I started walking, the back roads
quiet and slick, the puddles like little suns under the street-
lights. When I got home I didn't want to go inside, so I sat under
a maple tree in the overgrown backyard and listened to the
rain spattering the leaves, opening and closing my swollen hand,
trying not to cry. I know he was just a bird. I know that. But
he was the first good news we'd had in a year.

My sister thinks my father, in a drunken stupor, didn't see
Gary on the ground and stepped on him and threw his body in
the river. "You know he's a liar," she said, barging into my
room and waking me up. "He's a fucking liar that ruins everything he touches, and I'm gonna put it on his fucking tomb-
stone." She continued to poke holes in his story and pointed to
a spot on the porch and another on the bottom of his shoe.
Over coffee my brother said she's most likely right, and I
suppose she most likely is. But I for one want to give him the
benefit of the doubt. Because he, more than any of us, knows
what's at risk when you care about something. Because he
knew better and cared anyway. His heart's as good and dumb

as anybody's. And besides, "most likely right" is different than definite; "most likely right" leaves a little room for other possibilities. Just enough, it turns out, that every time I come across a telephone pole with a picture of a missing pet on it, or when I see an amber alert scroll across some road sign, my immediate sympathy gives way to something that feels better than bad, like my idiot heart is smirking, and I imagine Gary but grown-up, coasting the thermals, patrolling the patchwork fields, the Long Island Sound and the Great South—giant, and red, and terrible.

Everything Is a
Big Deal

We took a drive along Ocean Parkway and, like always, counted the rabbits on the side of the road. Twenty-seven, twenty-eight, twenty-nine. I blew into the mouth hole of the coffee cap, stuck my tongue in it, tipped up the cup until the tip of my nose touched the x in DIXIE and took a big sip.

"Thirty, thirty-one."

"Dead ones don't count," my father said.

"Thirty then."

Thirties one and two were on the far side of the Jones Beach roundabout as we circled the water tower and slingshotted ourselves back in the direction we'd just come from, like some kind of gravity-assist maneuver, the tug and pull of my latest fuckup forcing our return east. I had to be there at nine. I was nervous. I kept wondering if I would be looked down on, judged, made to clean toilets. Back then I had a friend who worked as a busboy in a local restaurant who told me about someone shitting in a urinal and wiping their ass with Italian bread. I didn't know what to expect.

By the time we exited onto the Robert Moses Causeway we were at fifty-seven live rabbits. My father dropped me in front of the old Cutting House a good ten minutes before the hour, and as I was getting out of his car he patted me on the shoulder, and I climbed out and closed the door and peered in through the open window. He was looking at me, right in the eyeballs.

"Call me if you got any problems."

"Thanks," I said, then tapped the roof of the car and walked inside. When I was sure he had pulled away I walked back out and smoked a cigarette and finished off my coffee, which had gone cold because I'd forgotten to drink it. Then I went back inside and down the hall to Jim Chapin's office, the Arboretum director, a short and thick cigar smoker with yellow-silver hair and a bum leg who—as I eventually figured from the betting slips on the floor of his pickup—spent most of everyday at the Bay Shore OTB. He didn't look up from his newspaper when I knocked on the already open door.

I cleared my throat. Nothing. "Hello," I said. Nothing. Nothing. Something—Jim shuffled, quickly looked me up and down, then returned to his paper. Without looking up again he said, "You're Albert?"

"Yes sir."

"Community service, right?"

"That's right."

"Five hundred hours?"

"Yep."

He folded his paper and slapped it down on the desk. Cigar ashes loop-de-looped out of the ashtray.

"Wanna tell me what happened?"

"Not really," I said, but then I told him all about it anyway.

I got my first car two weeks this side of seventeen: a rusted-out 1978 Toyota Land Cruiser FJ40, a four-speed manual straight six that got nine miles to the gallon and had holes in the floorboard big enough to dump cups of cold coffee through— including the cups—and where I lost pennies and cigarettes and one time a carnival goldfish in a plastic bag. What didn't rattle squeaked, it leaked antifreeze and oil, backfired on the downshift, and there was a crack in the windshield that I wanted to look like something—the east coast of Ireland or a vein in my father's forearm, a spider web even—but it didn't, it was just a big black crooked line from top to bottom that sometimes caught the light of the low morning sun on the way to school or the setting sun on the way home, or the headlights of an oncoming car. I wasn't good at wearing my seat belt or parking, stalled in stop-and-go and up-hills, and when it rained I liked to see how long I could go without using my wipers. I cursed men and the sun, stoplights and left-turners, Yankees bumper stickers and orange traffic cones. I middle-fingered slow ladies, and screwed up enough to be middle-fingered by them.

There were two bucket seats up front and a couple bench seats in the back that faced each other, and my mother made me drive my brother and a nice girl who lived a few houses

down—Kristy Klein, a chubby freshman who made her money
during lunch selling Jolly Ranchers for five cents each—to
school. For gas I charged them both six bucks a week that I
really spent on mini chocolate donuts and cigarettes. It was
almost summer, and the paper's five-day forecast was four
smiling suns and one with a little cloud on it, so I took the
hardtop off and stole my sister's sunglasses. With AJ sitting
shotgun and Kristy in the back putting her dark hair up in a
pink scrunchie, I'd just made the right onto Idle Hour Boulevard when a wonky triangle of mallards flew overhead on their
way to the river, and one of them dropped a Kelly-green-and-
white turd on the hood. Driver's side.

We all laughed, but after a while I told my brother and
Kristy to quit laughing, that it wasn't that funny, and when
they didn't quit laughing I yelled at them to quit laughing, and
when they didn't quit laughing again I swerved and ran over
some garbage cans because I was young then and had worse
impulse-control problems than I do now, also 'cause the cans
were right there and that's what occurred to me to do in that
Wednesday morning moment—Wednesday morning because
they were WRAP cans, beige with green tops. Recycle day.

The first one exploded newspapers into the air and rolled
right. The other was filled with bottles and cans and buckled
under the bumper and dragged a hundred-or-so feet before I
swerved across the street trying to lose it. I overcorrected, of
course, and came close to flattening a split-log fence on the
opposite side, the split-log posts sounding like someone spitting sunflower seeds as I passed them—*pth-pth-pth*—recalling
for me a long-ago summer day on the bench of a baseball dug-
out surrounded by friends, all of us sunburned and happy and

parodying our favorite players, which I suppose has something to do with why I failed to notice that Kristy had fallen out of the car until my brother hit me in the arm and screamed her name. I glanced in the rearview just in time to see her roll to a stop, then hobble off the road clutching her elbow before collapsing facedown on someone's front lawn. I drove a block and a half farther before pulling over, where my brother and I sat looking straight out the windshield not speaking for a while. Eventually he said, "We gotta go back."

I knew almost immediately that he was right, but still I sat there wondering how it was that a girl just fell out of my car, also about blame and seat belts and things that she could have but did not grab on to: the seat, the roll bar, the tailgate. I imagined she must have gone out like someone impersonating— poorly—a salmon, launching herself into the air, arms pinned to her sides, flopping and noiseless.

But no, yeah, AJ was right, we had to go back. "We gotta," he repeated. *But*, I thought again, but then nothing came after. I resigned myself to it, checked the mirrors, looked over my shoulder, signaled, and made a slow, careful, perfect three-point turn.

We heard her first, and when we were close enough to get a look at her, the left side of her face was scraped up but hadn't started bleeding yet, like someone had just scribbled on it with a rock, or scribbled on a rock with her. Her right arm was cut badly enough to make my legs wobbly, and I sat on the grass and watched some tree branches sway just a little in a just-a-little breeze. Soon enough the neighbors came out their front doors and crowded around, and someone called me a stupid son of a bitch, and a woman in pink pants squatted. A black sedan pulled over, followed by two police cars, a little later by an ambulance. I apologized and I apologized and I answered questions and said I was sorry, and they wrote things on pads while newspaper pages somersaulted a few feet down the road before lying flat again. Then I got arrested.

"She OK?" Jim said. "The girl?"

"Yeah, she's OK. Scraped up a little is all."

He nodded, satisfied. "OK then. So I got you for five hundred. Show up at nine and as long as you don't sleep under a tree you can leave at three and I'll give you eight hours."

"Thanks," I said. "Appreciate that."

"Guess you're waitin' for me to show you around the place," he said, then stood up and limped past me and out the door. I followed behind him in the hallway and watched him hobble toward the white pickup truck parked in the handicapped spot. On the side of the truck was a green maple leaf, and under it NEW YORK STATE OFFICE OF PARKS, RECREATION, HISTORIC PRESERVATION. Keys jingled. I walked around to the passenger side, and when I opened the door a Styrofoam cup fell out and rolled and hopped and tumble weed-ed across the parking lot. I chased it down, brought it back, climbed in, and saw the OTB slips all over the floor, watched the orange pine-tree air freshener swing from the rearview, the headliner yellowed from years of cigar smoke. I asked him if it would be OK if I had a cigarette. He looked at me sideways, gauged my age, said it'd be fine as long as I had one for him. I did, and he lit it, took a drag, blew smoke out his nostrils, and said, "I used to kill ducks. I'd soak bread in beer and feed it to them. After a few minutes they'd be pretty drunk. Then I'd just walk over and break their necks."

It was my father who picked me up at the police station. He didn't say a word, didn't even look at me, just signed some forms and walked out the double doors. I followed a safe distance behind him. He seemed large to me in a way that he hadn't in a while—the trouble I was in somehow reestablished his authority and physical size, or reestablished my lack of either. He seemed huge. Outside in the parking lot he stopped and waited till I caught up, put his hand on the back of my neck, squeezed, rubbed my head a little and said, "Tell your mother I yelled atcha."

Instead he took me to lunch at the Sayville Modern Diner with the little jukeboxes at each table and told me that when he was a kid, he and his buddy Ernie Fifer stole horses from Ryan's Stable in Bergen Beach. They headed north on Flatbush for a few miles before deciding on Florida—for the weather and girls—got halfway over the Brooklyn Bridge before they were caught. The two of them ended up in William E. Grady Vocational High School with car thieves and people who'd stabbed people. They loved it. After they graduated they joined the navy together. The both of them tested for sub school but Ernie got afraid, ended up a boatswain's mate on an aircraft carrier, was nineteen when he was swept off the deck in high seas.

The Bayard Cutting Arboretum sits on about seven-hundred acres and borders the west bank of the Connetquot River—

the same river I learned boats on—and Jim and I drove around its perimeter three slow times on the white gravel roads that encircle it, Jim giving me the history of the place as we went. I don't remember most of it, except that a large part of the park was destroyed by Hurricane Gloria in '85, and that cleanup took more than two years. I was more interested in how he'd hurt his leg, and when I had the chance, I asked him.

"I used to work tugs in Jamaica Bay," he said. "We were towing this sewage barge into the dumpsite there but it was overloaded, the barge, sat too low in the water and ran aground. The line snapped, and a rope movin' like that can cut a man in half. I'm lucky I still got the thing."

"How old were you?"

"Twenty-three. Now that dumpsite is the Riis public golf course."

I was about to tell him how my father lost his leg in a motorcycle wreck when Jim suddenly remembered where and why we were driving.

"That tree there is one of the largest Sergeant's weeping hemlocks in the world," he said. "And that one there's a weeping beech." We drove like that for an hour or so, him pointing to this and that, that and this, the pinetum, the hollies, the lilacs. Then, without saying anything, he drove to the gate and made a left onto Montauk Highway and headed into East Islip for an early lunch at some strip-mall bagel joint, where I ordered a sandwich of some kind and handed the guy a ten-dollar bill.

"Outta ten?"

I just stared at him. Eventually he gave me my change and not long after that my sandwich, which was wrapped in that white wax paper with one of those toothpicks with the red cellophane wig thing sticking out of it. We headed back, parked the truck in the southwest corner of the park near a pond with a little man-made waterfall that fed into the river. We ate with the doors open and the radio on, and watched the mallards and Canadian geese, a few mute swans, some of them with their feathered asses in the air feeding on plants below the surface.

When we finished, Jim showed me where the orange push mower was and gave me a red gas can and sent me out to a giant lawn scattered with black oaks. I obsessed over the lines the mower left in the grass, and took some joy in the dark green–light green–dark green of it all. I kept the lines as straight as possible, and if they weren't straight enough I'd go back over it a second time, sometimes a third. Around the black oak tree trunks I'd try for a perfect circle, three mower-widths thick. When I got tired I walked over to the bank of the river and envied the boats motoring by, then headed for a bench by the pond and watched the ducks and geese and swans for a few minutes. Eventually I got anxious about what Jim might say if he saw me there, so I got up, pushed the mower to the next section of lawn, and pulled the pull-cord.

The thing about juvenile traffic court is you just might get to hear a white woman tell the judge that she was riding her bicycle when she was hit in the face with a raw steak, which was thrown out the passenger-side window of a brown Chevrolet station wagon traveling in the opposite direction. The impact of the beef caused her to crash into the wooden golf clubs displayed outside Baker's Antiques and, after righting herself, she climbed back onto her bicycle and resumed peddling east on Montauk

to Hallmark Cards & Gifts, where she worked and where—
here she paused and started rubber-chinning—she washed her
face and telephoned the police. An anonymous someone had
already reported the license plate, which led to the arrest of
two seventeen year olds who I smoked a cigarette with on the
courthouse steps prior to heading in. The conversation I'd had
with them was unremarkable in every way, except that when
I asked the taller one what he did for work, he said he owned
a sixty-year-old retarded man. His buddy—who I nicknamed
Hot Eye because one lens of his glasses was fogged up—told the
judge he didn't mean to hit the lady in the face with the raw
steak, and the judge said "Baloney" with great authority.

Also unremarkable were the rest of the cases I heard that
day, including my own. The police officer's testimony was an
awful bore, just facts, and after he was through I was offered
the opportunity to say a few words in my defense. I said only
one, quietly, and to my shoes: "Sorry." The apology was met
with silence, and when I finally had the courage to look up at
the judge, he was blinking at me. Then he blinked at my father,
who was standing beside me, and asked him if he'd like to say
a few words on my behalf. Neither of us had expected this,
and it was cause for alarm. My father has never been good
with words—sometimes he isn't even decent with them. It's
not uncommon for my father, when asked what he'd like, to
struggle so violently with formulating a response that he fidg-
ets and his eyebrows move around weirdly, eventually becoming so flustered that he bites down on his tongue and turns a
little red before, finally, to everyone's terrific relief, he manages
to order the cheeseburger.

But somehow, without the slightest hesitation or twitch at

all my father looked at the judge and said, "Yeah your honor—uhhhhhh, I dunno . . . he's a kid, he took a hairy, you know? He's . . . gets good grades."

I watched the judge watch my father, and I could tell that he was somewhat confounded by what this man had just said to him. Then he shook his head, suspended my license, sentenced me to five hundred hours of community service, gaveled his gavel, and recommended I seek out a therapist.

"It's perfectly normal," my mother said later that night as she wiped the dinner table with a dirty blue dish sponge. "Everyone needs help sometimes." But I refused therapy, and would continue to until a few years after she died, when a different judge in a different state didn't give me the option.

I woke up around eight thirty the next morning, and even though we were running late my mother took me to the Oakdale Deli, bought me a BLT and a soda for lunch, a coffee for right then. I was nervous about being late, but when we got there a note was scotch-taped to the office door.

Al,

Mow.

—Jim

I mowed. Around noon I got hungry, and I sat on that bench by that pond and watched the ducks and geese and swans again, then figured I'd cut them a break and broke off the corners of my sandwich. They raced to eat what little there was, and I spoke words of encouragement to the less aggressive ones, made a game of trying to get them their share until a swan swam over and chased them away. I gave it the finger, then walked back to the mower and continued staining my sneakers green.

The next day I saw the same note on Jim's door, did the same thing. I saw the same note all week, did the same thing all week, except I started buying an extra roll for twenty-five cents to feed the ducks and geese, and made a game of not feeding the swans. Soon enough I was buying two rolls. Then I got a new note.

A—

Keep mowing.

—*J.*

I kept mowing, kept watching the boats on the river, kept feeding the fowl at lunch, was at my bench with a sandwich when I heard quacking and honking, wings moving. I looked up and watched some mallards half-fly, half-run on top of the water and splash back down. Their webbed-feet footprints rippled out in concentric circles on the surface of the pond, and I followed them back to where they started, where I saw one duck bobbing back and forth with no head. Like, its head was missing. I stood up at the water's edge to see if I wasn't seeing it correctly, but I was—its head was gone. I walked around the pond to get a closer look, then returned to my bench and fed the ducks and geese and even the swans.

A few days later Jim pulled up in his truck, beeped the horn, and asked me how it was going.

"Good," I said. "Where you been?"

"My office," he said.

"Right," I said. "Got it." Then I told him about the headless duck. He stared at my nose for a second, then smiled, said it was probably an alligator snapping turtle.

"They're like dinosaurs, these things. They get big—up to a hundred pounds big—and they sit there, half buried in the mud, with their mouths open. There's this little lure thing that hangs off their tongues, and if anything gets close to it, like, for example, a feeding duck with its little duck ass in the air, it'll bite its head clean off and—*bloop*—up floats the duck."

"Wow," I said. "That's something."

"No it isn't," he said, easing off the brake, slowly pulling away.

EAT THE MILK

For my brother's twenty-fourth birthday I bought him a little plastic horsey doll that came with a little plastic orange comb so you could little-plastic-orange-comb its mane and tail and shiny coat, but before I could mail it to him my grandmother peeled the medicinal transdermal patch off her body and ate it. It put her in the emergency room followed by six weeks' recovery in Bay Shore's Petite Fleur Nursing Home, so I arranged for some time off from the marina I was working at and drove the ten hours north to my parents' house, but my mother forgot to leave the key under the rock in the garden, which was never really a garden as much as it was a rock and a frog in a top hat lawn ornament hanging out in some weeds. Across the way, on the other side of the cement path that curved between the driveway and the back door, near a bush that had some-how survived decades of laundry water that shot out of a yellowing PVC pipe sticking out of a half-buried basement window, was a small, grayed square of warped plywood with a broken red brick on top of it. Underneath that were some earthworms and pill bugs and a stubbed-out cigarette filter.

I walked a counterclockwise lap around the outside of the house and found a Styrofoam cooler on the porch with no key in it, and a dirty white sock in the bushes near the driveway with no key in it, and the key was not in the barbeque either, or the mailbox or newspaper box, or the bird feeder hanging cracked and crooked from the white-and-brown branch of the dying birch slanting outside the hall window. The key was also not in the gutter on the southwest corner of the house stopped up with at least five falls' worth of oak leaves and pine needles, or under the potted daisy outside the garage. I lit a cigarette, covered my left eye with my left hand, and called my mother a dick. Then I busted out a screen and clambered through the open kitchen window.

My belt buckle was a problem for me, and in trying to work it over the window ledge I bumped a ceramic figurine of a little boy with abnormally large eyes holding a MOMMIES ARE #1 sign that I'd bought for her at the Idle Hour Elementary School fair in the fourth or fifth grade, and its head broke off when it hit the counter. Sparkles came bounding into the room and, when I was finally inside and upright, I squatted down to pet her. She hopped up on her hind legs to lick my face, then pushed off and spun and pointed her asshole at me. When I hesitated a second, she eye-contacted me over her shoulder like *C'mon already*, so I pet and scratched around her asshole, saying, "Hi, girl, OK, girl, OK . . ." until her back legs buckled and the right one started flailing around involuntarily, her toenails tapping the tile in a bell curve of sound—slow, fast, slow.

I stood and got her a doggie treat out of the drawer, which I think she swallowed whole, then she stayed staring up at me, hoping for another.

"Sparkles," I said, "I love you, but I can't give you any more snacks. You're too fuckin' fat. Keep it up and you're gonna get diabetes, dude, and then your life will be fuckin' snackless, and what kind of life is a snackless life? Next thing you know they're amputating your legs off, and then you're a baby walrus for real, only you suck at swimming and would probly drown in your own water bowl. Probly have to strap you to a skateboard with bungee cords and drag your fat self to the vet. Dude'll take one look and be like, 'Guess she has a gland problem?' And I'll be like, 'No, a snack problem.' And he'll be like, 'Oh, well how about this snack?' And you know what that snack is, Sparkles? A syringeful of poison. Then you're fuckin' dead, dude. Forever. There's no snacks when you're dead. So do us both a favor—scram."

After a short standoff, she licked my pant leg.

So I gave her another treat because I'm a sucker for dogs, and when she finished with that one she tried for a third, and I gave her a third because I'm a sucker for dogs multiple times. I almost gave her a fourth, but instead I blew smoke in her face and she blinked and twitched and turned and sauntered away, every now and again casting glances back at me over her shoulder until she was under the table, where she lay down and closed her eyes to dream of food in black-and-white. I put the cigarette out in the sink and opened another window.

On the kitchen table was a note from my mother that hoped my drive was good and if I was hungry there were cold cuts in the fridge and don't smoke in the house and she saw Gloria Estefan at Jones Beach last weekend and it was a great show. She would be home from work around five and she couldn't wait to see me and the doctors found cancer in Grandma's kidney, don't worry, XOXO. I lit another cigarette. It was 3:32.

By 4:16 I had eaten all the cold cuts and bacon and some pizza bagels and pierogies and a strawberry fruit-at-the-bottom yogurt and felt a little sick, so I lay down on the couch in the den and turned on the TV to a show about a lady judge whose veins popped out of her forehead while she yelled. I watched thinking she wouldn't be so mean if there wasn't a big black bailiff standing there with a gun and a club protecting her— three minutes of that and I was overcome with restlessness. Somewhere along the way I'd become incapable of relaxing, of allowing my body to be still, of rest. It isn't that I have more energy than I know what to do with, because I don't. It's that my body is uncomfortable. It's not pain, necessarily, but an antsy annoyance of the muscles and—when still—I become excruciatingly aware of just how uncomfortable I am. Then I have to move. I get up and pace around, shake my hand like I just touched something too hot, fidget, tap a table or countertop. I take long walks.

In a car, though, I'm stuck, and the entire drive up from Wilmington had been a nonstop series of seat adjustments and shoulder rolls, opening and closing windows, switching CDs and tinkering with the volume knob, rubbing my eyeballs and punching myself in the legs, as if hurting the leg hurts the ache that's in it. I smoked a lot of cigarettes, cracked my knuckles, my ankles, my back and my neck, cracked everything that was crackable and bobbed my head in order to make a smashed bug on the windshield appear to fly just above the treetops bordering the interstate, until I banged my chin on the steering wheel while attempting to clear a particularly tall pine outside of Richmond. When that got old, I looked for things to look at: the rearview, the rearview, trees, a dead dog next to a blue hospital sign and GOD BLESS OUR SOLDIERS BEEFY BURRITO $1.39, the rearview—anything but the road itself. I've been in over a dozen accidents, all of which were my fault. I hit a bridge once. I drove through a closed garage door. It's stopping I have a problem with.

I got up from the couch, wrote a note on the back of my mother's note, took the horsey doll, and headed off to see my grandmother.

The nursing home parking lot was filled with cars that looked alike, except for a running ambulance with two EMTs leaning on it. I smiled at my shoes as I passed them, walked around to the front, where three women in wheelchairs were feeding gray-purple pigeons, and felt a little guilty when I heard their squeaky wings and realized I'd scared them off. I apologized to the woman closest to me, who had eyes like two copper coins floating in fog.

As I made my way down a long hallway I passed the activities board, and the week was jam-packed with Balloon Tennis and Music-and-Motion and Let's Make Oriental Fans, Pet Visits and Grandma's Handbag and *Elizabeth Rafter turns*

101 years old!!! At the reception desk a book lay open with four columns—Name, Date, Time, Visiting—and behind it a white nurse in pink scrubs sat not smiling with a half-eaten sandwich in front of her. I said hello and asked her if it was a turkey sandwich.

"Ham," she said.

I didn't believe her. Then I asked her if she could tell me where my grandmother was and she asked me if I could spell my grandmother's last name. I could and did, and she looked it up on her computer—typey typey typey, return—told me her room was B10 but that she might be in the dining hall, then took half of the half of sandwich in one bite.

B2, B4, B6, B8—I thought of Battleship, my favorite childhood game. My brother liked Connect Four and used to lick the leftover Italian dressing off his salad plate. My grandmother wasn't in her room, but her roommate was, in bed, her body bent and twisted with MS or some other awful thing, her mouth open to the cracks in the ceiling. I said hello and she said nothing at all, and above her bed hung a painting of Jesus Christ floating up to heaven, topless and staring directly into the camera, his arms spread wide like, *Behold, cameraman . . . I'm flying!* Another possibility, it seemed to me, was that he was fleeing, and I imagined knocking him out of the sky with a rock.

Nailed to the wall above my grandmother's bed was a small wooden crucifix and pictures of my dead grandfather and their children and their children's children—the same picture that hung in our hallway of my brother, sister, and me naked in a bathtub together, which probly saved time but doesn't seem like any way to get clean. I said goodbye to my grandmother's roommate, then waved bye at her, then felt dumb about it and walked out.

Wandering around the hallways I overheard an old man report to a nurse that another man "killed me on the back of the leg six days ago," and a woman using a dirty-tennis-balled walker was staring into a fish tank to apply light red lipstick. I stopped at the front desk again, and the now sandwichless nurse pointed me toward the dining hall, a large room with six or seven long tables in it. It was full but quiet except for the TV and a lady rocking violently hollering for someone-or-thing named Mashtar, and as I looked from face to face it occurred to me that women make the mistake of living too long more than men do.

My grandmother was seated at the table farthest from the window, pinching her paper bib and staring at the wall. I walked over and put a smile on my face so fake it trembled. She had a see-through mustache and the hairs were longer at the corners of her mouth. I kissed her forehead.

"What's up, Grams, heard you ate your medicine patch."

"Sydney?"

"No . . . I'm your daughter's son. Alby."

Something inside her shifted, she shook, and her eyes wandered off, following butterflies or parakeets or the word *pajamas* ticker-taping across her eyeballs, a monkey riding a dog or pink fighter jets on their way to kill kill kill. Or more likely they were following nothing at all, which at that moment was somewhere on the white wall between the clock and the television advertising deodorant. *Smell cool.*

Her eyes went wide. "Everything's getting weird."

"It's always been weird. Here's a horsey doll."

I took her shaking, spotted hand and tried to put the doll in it, but she wouldn't take it, so I placed it on the table in front of her.

"Don't eat the comb," I said.

She reached out and knocked the horsey doll over, then recoiled her shaking hand in a way that reminded me of a vacuum cleaner cord retracting.

"It's OK," I said. "It's just a toy."

She looked off, and after a while I waved my hand in front of her face. "Grandma," I said, snapping my fingers now. "Hello? Yoo-hoo."

She looked at me and flashed her gums in what I think was a smile.

"The pope came," she said.

"On a kid's back?"

I half-regretted it almost immediately, because who am I to insult something that gave her comfort? I'm all for painkillers, just prefer mine in pill form. Pints and rocks glasses. Ladies.

"He said . . . everybody should speak English . . ."

"Don't popes speak Latin," I said, "and like, refer to themselves in the first person plural? *We am the Harriet Tubman of pedophiles.* Did We explain We's hostility toward women, gaylords, and science? How about common-sense issues like condoms as a way of preventing AIDS and, you know, not allowing priests to rape children's buttholes and mouths? Did We say anything about that, Grandma? Because I think that We—never mind."

I half-regretted that almost immediately, too, but before I could apologize she started singing a song in Italian or Nonsense, I couldn't tell the difference, just sat there listening to her until the antsy feeling I get settled somewhere in my chest and

I felt like moving again. I stood up to leave, but something about the smallness of her voice—the pitch, my inability to understand her, the helplessness of it—made me feel lonely for her. So I resolved to stay at least until my mother showed up, and I sat back down as four nurses in pink scrubs wheeled in four carts stacked with orange trays of food. It wasn't long before my grandmother stopped singing, and then we just sat there quietly, she staring at her special spot on the wall, me at the TV, watching the end of a commercial where a young girl on a beach goes, "I need a brownie . . ." and then all her friends chime in with, *"Oh yeah, she's menstrual!"* and laugh.

Eventually a tray was placed on the table in front of us, on it a dish of pureed meat and what I think was pureed rice, a bowl of something orange, red Jell-O, a glass of thickened water, a glass of thickened milk, and a cup of thickened tea.

"Will you be feeding her today?" asked the nurse.

"I'd rather not," I said, and she gave me this look, so I said, "I'd better not," and she gave me the same look as before, in fact I don't think she ever changed it, so I said I'd try.

I started with the meat because it was the most brown, which seemed important. I took a heaping spoonful, asked, "Ready?" and as my grandmother said yes I stuck it in. She coughed and spit up on her chin. "Wup," I said, and wiped it off with the bib.

I'm sure at one point it looked as if I was trying to feed her left cheek. At another, her nostrils. I flicked tea off her shoulder. But soon enough we found our rhythm, Grandma and me, and we settled into it. I'd scoop a heaping spoonful of something, hold it up in front of her so she could see it, then announce what I thought it was. "Rice," I'd say. "I think this is rice." Then I'd slowly bring it to her lips and wait until she parted them. I'd slide the spoon and its contents in and tip it up until she'd close her mouth around it. Then I'd draw the spoon out and watch her jaw as she swished the stuff around before swallowing. It was strangely satisfying, our method. It meant there was an understanding. Sometimes I think all I ever want is an understanding.

After twenty or so messy minutes I'd spooned in everything except the milk. I felt proud about this. I was excited to tell my mother. See, Ma? I'm helpful. I'm a good boy. Then I considered her note, my watch, did math. She should be here already, I thought. Any minute.

Grandma, I said. Eat this. Eat it. It's milk. Eat the milk. You need milk, milk's good for you. Eat it. Eat the milk. Grams. Grandma. Hey. Grandma. Grandma. Grams. Grandma. Eat this for strength. Eat it. It's milk. Eat it. Eat this. Eat the milk. Eat the milk the pope said eat the milk. The pope loves the milk. Eat it. Eat the milk.

But she just kept turning her head from it, side to side to side, and when she brought her shaking, spotted hand up to push it away, I faked left and went right and snuck it in there, through lips and over tongue, no teeth to stop me. She immediately coughed and retched and began throwing up a jelly rainbow just as my mother walked through the door with a big smile on her face that meant *hello how are you I've missed you I know you smoked in the house and what's with the broken statue*, then seeing my vomiting grandmother went, "Ooooooh," and nurses scattered, and someone called out for paper towels and repeated, "Paper towels!" and somebody else started patting my grandmother's back, and somebody else got locked out of their house because somebody else didn't leave the key, and somebody else bought the deodorant and somebody else bought whatever that girl on the beach was selling, tampons probably, and somebody else is dying because somebody else is always dying, people are always suffering and dying, and I just sat there holding the spoon, smiling nervously and then laughing nervously and then just laughing, and then laughing so hard my eyes started to water and everything got blurry, and none of it was funny at all.

THE BLOCK, TWICE

I once dated this girl who was skinny and flat-chested and could tap dance. Her name was Carey and she had a tiny lower jaw. When she was younger some of her bottom teeth had to be pulled to make room for the rest, and those came in crooked, pointed in different directions—maybe that's why she dropped out of college. She waited tables at an expensive restaurant, made pretty good money. When she doodled, she doodled barns. She had blond hair and blond eyebrows, little blond hairs on her fingers, drove a blue Suzuki Sidekick. When she would come over I'd kiss her on her lip-glossed lips and say, "What's up? How's your blue Suzuki Sidekick? You're my sidekick so why don't you go tap dance on my kitchen floor." She'd giggle. "I'm serious," I'd say, and I was. I loved watching her tap dance, her little legs going, her little black shoes clicking louder than they should in celebration of nothing or everything in particular.

On weekend nights I'd go to the restaurant she worked at and drink at the bar. After she clocked out she'd sit next to me and we'd talk and pinch each other's legs and stomachs, hold hands, watch how much the other servers tipped-out the bus-boys, whisper about injustice over discounted liquor and free chicken. Sometimes fish. Sometimes Joey, a lanky white kid who washed dishes, would come out front for a few minutes and rap for us, make words rhyme that didn't—*I'm a hellion, explore vaginas like Magellian*—things like that. We'd hang out till the place would close up, eleven or twelve or four a.m. depending on I don't know what, then we'd go back to my apartment, where I'd put on some ragtime and sit on the floor, watch her tap dance on the white tiles of my kitchen, applaud and cheer, laugh, shout nice things. "Better than Ben Vereen!" I'd yell, tackle her and take her clothes off, have unprotected sex with her for a minute.

The dessert chef at the restaurant was Billy Something, and Billy Something made a terrific baked Alaska and an OK crème brûlée and a weird-looking face when I staggered through the double doors of the kitchen late one night and grabbed him by his white coat collar and slammed him into the wall and said stop rubbing my girlfriend's shoulders you fuckin' dickhole. He had also turned Carey on to coke, but that didn't bother me nearly as much as the fact that he felt comfortable rubbing her shoulders in my presence, and that she seemed to like it. I was still shaking him when Joey and this other guy whose name I can't remember but he had thick eyelashes, they hooked me by the armpits and dragged me outside, the whole time asking me if I was cool.

"You cool? You cool? You cool?"

"No," I said, "I'm not cool. Stop asking me if I'm cool . . . asking me if I'm cool is making me not-cooler."

They lit me a cigarette, lit themselves cigarettes, pep-talked me and told me to wait, left me sitting alone on a concrete square around a magnolia tree. I talked to myself about cannolis and motherfuckers while I pitched pieces of bark mulch at a brick wall. I spit and zipped my jacket's zipper up and down and up, down and up, down, waited. Carey never came out.

The front door of the place was glass and locked. I knocked on it. I cupped my hands over my eyes and looked in, but I couldn't see anybody. I pressed my ear to it. Knocked some more and waited, re-sat and waited, re-stood and knocked on the door again. I pounded on it. Yelled *hey* at it. Yelled *Carey* at it until the owner and head chef, James Morris—still thin and I never understood how a chef could be thin—he walked up on the other side of the door and said, "You should go home, Alby."

"Where's Carey?"

We stared at each other through fingerprint smudges.

"You should go home."

I knew he was looking out for me, but I told him that if he didn't open the door I'd punch his entire family in the face, and that when I punched his mom in the face, I'd punch her in the forehead during a family photograph, and then I'd have it framed by a professional so that I could hang it on the wall above my couch and look at it every day and smile. He walked away. I paced, talked to myself, sat Indian-style on the concrete square around the magnolia tree. I stood up, knocked on the door, and shouted for Joey until he peeked his head around the corner and walked over.

"Hey man."

"Hey man."

"What's she doing?"

"Nothin'," he said. "Everybody's just having drinks. You should probly get outta here. Wait for things to blow over."

I said all right, I'll leave, but I'm out of cigarettes and would he give me one. He said he would and I said thanks man, and he reached into his shirt pocket for his pack and took out a cigarette, unlocked the door and opened it a crack, stuck the cigarette through. I took it and put it in my mouth, patted my pockets, said I needed a light. He took out his lighter and cracked the door a bit farther, and I lunged and wedged my face in there, got my left leg in, too, before he pulled it closed on me and started yelling for help. Then I started yelling for help. Then I yelled for Carey. Then I yelled, "Just talk to me," and "Please," and "Don't do this to me," and "Please," and "Please," and *Please!*" and "Ow!" and "Fuck you Billy you're a scumbag and your desserts aren't good!" James and that other guy whose name I can't remember with the eyelashes came running over and helped Joey push me out, locked the door, threatened to call the police if I didn't leave. "Good," I said. "Call the fuckin' police. I'll fuckin' . . . You guys are assholes." Then I sat on the concrete square and caught my breath, smoked half a cigarette and went home, called Carey and left a message. Then I called her again and left a message again, called her again and hung up, took a shit and cried, called her again and left another message. She never called me back.

I still have a magic marker drawing she made for me when we were together. It's a lawn and flowers and the sun is in the upper left-hand corner and in the middle of the air she wrote in purple: *Have a great day, Alby! Love, Carey.* I had it hanging on my refrigerator with a magnet for a few months afterward. Then I put it in a cardboard box with old soccer trophies and a Space Camp graduation plaque.

My sister called the same day I got a toothache, said she ran into Carey in the city and stopped to talk to her. Apparently she was doing really well in advertising and getting married to a banker guy. I asked her if she asked about me. Nope, my sister said. Not at all. Then she went on about politics and the media for a while. It went like: "Fuckin' . . . resistance diminishes as commercial interruptions amplify, you know? Like, they're pumping so much bullshit it serves as some sort of static. TV, satellites, laptops, live-feed Internet . . . we've got all this access but as a society we're becoming distanced further from the war and the humanness required to fully fuckin' experience it. I mean . . . we've landed on Mars but aren't intellectually that far from painting on cave walls."

"Antelopes and shit."

"What?"

"On the cave walls."

"Anyway. The big lie of the television age is that we're better informed, when really what we're shown is what we're told is important, and we think it's important cause it's what we're being shown."

"Right," I said. "How does Carey look?"

"She looks great."

"You're an asshole," I said and hung up on her. Then I

walked around the block, twice. I noticed things. Cars have wheels. The wood on that house is painted red. That fire hydrant is there in case there is a fire nearby. I haven't had a girlfriend in two years. Trees.

On Biltmore there was a sprinkler sprinkling an arc of water onto the street and a squirrel on a birch branch. It jumped to a pine branch. It ran up the branch, down the trunk, out another branch, and jumped to a split-log fence post. It ran along the fence, then down the fence, then jumped to the ground. It ran around a little, then stopped and stood on its back legs, looked around. It ran and stopped and looked, ran and stopped and looked. Ran some more and stopped some more. Looked some more. Ran into the street and almost got run over by a red car. The driver didn't even slow down. My tooth started to throb. I walked to a bar.

There was a paper sign in the window hanging from a piece of string, swaying and spinning, rocking back and forth in ceiling-fan air, advertising nothing in particular, just: LUCKY DAY. I liked it. I went inside and had a few drinks and then a few more and then spotted a girl down the bar to my right. She had pale skin and pink ears that she tucked her black hair behind, wore white on her eyelids like in the fifties. Each time I looked at her my chest hurt in new and exciting ways. I kept drinking and looking and considering approaches:

Stare at her. Keep staring at her until she notices. Wave.

Write her a three-napkin love letter. Begin: *Dear Lady, I really like your hairdo, and your makeup is great.* Then use words that show you are nice.

Wait by the ladies' room. When she walks by, stop her and say, "Sorry buddy, that's the women's bathroom." She will feel less confident.

Wait by the ladies' room. Follow her in. Kiss her with force and passion. Tell her her lips taste delicious and pin her against the wall. Take her clothes off and pinch her nipples, lick her nipples, suck one like it's a lemonade cigar. Drop to your knees and hike her right leg onto your shoulder. Ask, "That a birthmark?" "It's a mole." "Oh." Kiss her pussy, lick her pussy, finger fuck it like you're mad at it, like it's on the other side of the room and you have to tell it a secret, your index finger curling c'mere c'mere c'mere. Stop, ask her name, how do you spell that? Spell it with your tongue till she comes. Take your dick out, jerk it off a little, make a noise like an injured cow, stand up and fuck her. Get her pregnant with twin retards, pull your pants up and run out. Walk back in and tell her you might love her but probably not, wash your hands with soap, check your hair and your teeth, run back out. Go to 7-Eleven and buy a snack.

Instead, I got very drunk and don't remember speaking to anyone that night, or leaving, and I woke up on my kitchen floor next to an unopened box of fish sticks. My tooth was ringing. I stood up and tongued it. It kept ringing. I moved to the bathroom and picked up a cap-less tube of the stuff with fluoride and the sonic toothbrush my mother had given me for Christmas a few years before. Brushing didn't help. Mouthwash didn't help. Floss made me bleed, and didn't help. I spat in the sink and the brown-red blood on porcelain was roughly in the shape of South America. I turned on the faucet and watched it spin down and away. I took a piss and flushed, watched it spin down and away. I ate aspirins and called the dentist, said it was an emergency, and they said I could come in the following morning at ten. I baked the fish sticks, ate some, and took a nap. That night I went back to the bar.

That sign was there again, and that girl was there again, and I drank drinks and considered approaches again. Then I quit considering anything at all and walked over not knowing what I would say, which was hello. She turned around and I felt like a hose in my chest kinked. Then it unkinked.

"I think you're really pretty," I said. "Got a boyfriend?"

She leaned back and squinted at me. "No," she said. "I don't."

"I'll date the hell out of you," I said. "I'll date you so hard you'll puke. Wanna go on a date sometime? We could do something."

She smiled and blinked and stirred her drink with her drink straw and said, "You know you asked me out last night, right?"

"Oh." I looked her down and up. "Well . . . what'd you say last night?"

"I said no."

"Oh." I stood there awkwardly for a few seconds, then apologized for bothering her again.

I was already walking away when she said, "You're cute, but you shouldn't drink so much." I kept walking, weaved between people on my way to the men's room where I pissed two-handed figure eights into the urinal, the intersection crossing an X on the blue urinal cake. A guy came in and started pissing at the urinal next to me and pushed out a fart that whispered *Ppppert-Pppplussss*. I nodded. On the wall in front of me in black marker was written SUCK MY BLOATED LOVE KNOB FAGGOT. Underneath that someone wrote *fuck you* with an arrow pointing to FAGGOT, and then a third person with a blue marker scribbled out the tip of that arrow and looped it around so that *fuck you* pointed to itself.

I shook and tucked, zipped and flushed, washed my hands and dried my hands on my shirt and walked out and into the bar and out the front door.

I went home, slept for four hours, woke up at six. I made some coffee, took a sip, spit it out in the sink, and tongued my tooth for a while. I sat in the sun on the porch till nine, then walked the three miles to the dentist. On the way I saw a woman walking in the opposite direction with a brown dog. Inside my skull: There goes another living organism on a piece of rope.

The dentist's office was in a strip mall between Mr. Video and Angel Tips Nail Salon. I walked in and people were scattered around the waiting room, reading magazines. *Better Homes and Gardens. Cosmopolitan. Us. Time.* I walked over to the counter. The receptionist was on the telephone, and she pointed to a clipboard. A blue pen was tied to it with a piece of green floss, and as I was signing in she asked me if I had ever been there before. When I told her I hadn't she handed me a stack of forms to fill out: Date, Age, Sex, Height, Weight, In Case of Emergency Contact, two pages of Medical History (Question 8: *Do you bruise easily?*), one-page Patient Information Sheet, one-page Arbitration Agreement, one-page Patient Acknowledgment of Dental Materials Fact Sheet, one-page

Patient Acknowledgment of Notice of Privacy Practice. I sat in the lobby for a long time until a woman mispronounced my last name and led me to a white room where a Mexican man with cut-up knuckles X-rayed my head. When he was finished, the same woman led me to another white room. I sat in there for a long time, stared at a crack in the ceiling and wondered if Carey ever thinks about me. When the dentist finally came in I was glad.

She was older, pale and pretty, thin to the point of delicate-looking, had a mole on her left eyelid. I'd date her, big-time. She said hello and asked how I was, looked through a folder, put on rubber gloves. She was very polite.

She adjusted a surgical mask and goggles and my chair and the light. She arranged metal things on a metal tray. "OK," she said, "let's have a look." She opened my tooth without a local and poked at it with a metal toothpick, asking, "Does this hurt?"

"Yes."

"Does this hurt?"

"Yes."

"Does this hurt?"

Yes.

AMERICAN NINJA 2

My brother bet me five hundred dollars she wouldn't make it past December. I accepted and won—Grandma died January third. I took time off work and went home to help my mother with funeral arrangements, but mostly I ate snacks and watched shitty movies. After *American Ninja 2* I got up from the couch and kicked a bag of microwave popcorn. Unpopped kernels went everywhere.

I did a cartwheel into the kitchen and looked at food in the refrigerator and thought about my grandmother's dentures. They were yellowed and ugly and shifted in her mouth, and I wondered why the dentist didn't make them pretty and white. Realism, I guessed, the truthful treatment of material. Here's some more: V. C. Andrews romance novels are popular, the dentist hurts, and Q-tips get yellow when you clean your ears. The dog waddled by and I imagined cutting her in half with a sword.

I grabbed the two-liter bottle of Coke, put the bottle on the table, unscrewed the cap, walked over to the cabinet, got a glass out of the cabinet, put the glass on the table, picked up the bottle, poured some Coke into the glass, paused, looked at the dog—who was looking at me—while I waited for the fizz to go away, topped off the glass, put the bottle down on the table, picked up the glass, drank half, put the glass down, thought about my grandmother, and punched the bottle off the table. Sparkles licked puddles of cola.

I sat down, at the same table where I used to eat sweet breakfast cereals with 2% milk while listening to the sound of my mother's high heels click the floor as she got me ready for school. I thought the Poconos were Caribbean islands back then. After school my brother and I toasted Ellio's pizzas and talked about the pretty girls we liked to watch chewing sandwiches and drinking juice boxes through straws. Every Thursday night the white bags of drive-thru McDonald's sat next to the sink, every Friday night a grease-stained box of Chinese from Wing Wah Kitchen. It is the table where I admitted to my father that I was afraid of porcelain dolls, and the table where my mother admitted to me, after her second coffee mug of Fu-Ki plum wine, that her father was a fucking asshole who killed stray cats with a shovel when they wandered into his backyard.

My grandmother died in this kitchen, near a toaster full of pizza bagels that weren't quite ready, ten days after her asshole grandson, me, had given her a *Dance Your Pants Off!* workout video for Christmas. Her mouth was open and there was shit in her diaper. My mother found her.

I was the first one back, eager to help, less disturbed by the

death of my grandmother—we had expected it for years—
than by the note on the table asking me if I would clean up
my crumbs and vacuum the den before my brother arrived.
He was flying into JFK and my mother had gone to pick him
up. The note set me off, and so while Sparkles was pink-tonguing
brown puddles, I turned and threw my empty glass at the toaster,
threw the toaster at the microwave, picked it up by the cord,
walked into the hall swinging it over my head, and smashed it
into the bookcase shelving my mother's favorites—*Women
Who Love Too Much*; *Womanspirit Rising*; *Too Good for Her
Own Good*; *Only the Strong Survive*; *If It Hurts, It Isn't Love*;
Loving the Self-Absorbed . . . I wonder if she bought all those
thinking of me, or my brother, or my father, or her father,
or all of us. I was still kicking the thing when Sparkles came
bounding in, pounced on it, bit the cord, shook her head, and
dragged it around the room. We had a little tug of war before
she rolled on her back, exposing her belly. Her vulnerability
made something in me ache to hurt her.

I decided it would be best if I left the house.

I'll describe the walls because that's easy—they were white,
and I hurt my right pinky knuckle punching some of them
while I walked through rooms searching for my car keys. My
inability to find them frustrated me so badly that I beat up the
bathroom door, limped away and waved my fist at the plaster
statue of Beethoven's head on top of the piano we never learned
to play. After all that, I found the keys in a coat pocket I had
already checked but somehow missed. I grabbed the video and
made toward the back door, but on my way I noticed Sparkles
cowering under the kitchen table, shaking, terrified of me. I
hated myself a little extra, fed her a slice of manufactured

cheese, patted her on the head, and took the back steps three at a time.

At the bottom I picked up a stick and swung it around because I liked the noise and then I threw it at a leafless tree and missed. I opened the door of my car—a black Camry with a cracked back bumper and a wire coat hanger for an antenna—climbed in, and slammed it closed. The window handle fell off. When I started the car Justin Timberlake sang "Cry Me a River" and I wanted to kick him out a skyscraper window like Clapton's kid; watch him fall from far away like 9/11 victims.

On Woodlawn Avenue I saw a mailbox painted like a cow. On Idle Hour Boulevard I saw a mailbox shaped like a swan. On Shore Drive I did math with mailbox numbers until the 7-Eleven on the corner of Vanderbilt and Montauk. There was a telephone pole with two signs stapled to it. One read:

NO INSURANCE?
CHEAP DENTAL CARE
1 800 DENTALL
1324 Lincoln Drive

The other was an invitation to a Mormon open house.

I pulled into the 7-Eleven and bought coffee and cigarettes and sat on the curb and smoked two and thought it through. I'd show up at the open house and knock on the door and say hello. Once inside I would do drugs and gamble and have sex with a hooker. Then I would give a lecture on evolution, do a scientific experiment (something with a Bunsen burner), accuse them of mental imperialism, and kill everyone there. I would punch noses and poke eyes out and smash teeth out of skulls. I would walk on tables and jump off and kick heads. I'd grab everyday objects in the room and throw them at faces, pinch ladies' asses, and shove a small person into something sharp. I'd duck and weave and block slow punches, dodge lunges, light fires, insult children and mustaches. I'd read three paragraphs of *Fishboy* and use page fifty-six to paper-cut throats, kick stomachs and brush my teeth, crack spines and comb my hair, break necks and do long division. I'd poison like four of them. I'd breathe through a florescent-colored snorkel—a pink one maybe—and I'd keep a pretty lady alive to fold my clothes. If she didn't do a good job I'd bite her white arm. It would look like the teeth marks in a Styrofoam coffee cup. I took another sip.

I stood up, lit a third cigarette, and threw the burning book of matches into the garbage bin. I watched from the car—black smoke, melting plastic, charred Slurpee cups and candy wrappers, half-eaten hot dogs, and flame swirled up and blackened then shattered the ten-by-ten-foot front window. I felt better, and it was only 2:32 p.m.

I pulled out of the parking lot and headed east down Montauk Highway and saw the West Sayville fire trucks speeding in the opposite direction. I watched telephone poles and small leafless trees blur by. I passed an Exxon and a Gulf and a Texaco and a Shell. The world is full of shit and gasoline. I passed lube joints and fast-food huts, nail salons and pizza places, pharmacies and Old Navys. I thought about the American landscape and punching Morgan Fairchild in the face.

I passed Highway Call Box 5-492.

I passed a bank.

I passed a man hitchhiking.

This one does not end with me at a bar, or me at a bar and losing a fist fight, or me at a bar and talking to my father, or me at a bar and angry, or me at a bar and really drunk, or me getting thrown out of a bar for being really drunk, although I'm confident at least one of those did happen after the funeral. This story ends at Mr. Video.

I returned *American Ninja 2* and put a shiny quarter into a giant gumball machine hoping to get a green one, which equals a free rental. If I don't get green I like white ones because they don't discolor your teeth. I thought about my grandmother's dentures as I listened to the gumball spiral down and spiral down and spiral down and clink. Yellow.

MAKING NICE

I must have been five or six when my father and I were walking outside Mario's Barber Shop and I looked up and wanted to hold his hand but could only fit mine around his thumb, so I kicked him. At eight years old I beat up my brother because he took his watch off and the band smelled like Cheez Doodles. At eleven I killed a seagull with a rock and at twelve I killed a lot of them with a Crosman BB gun. I got my driver's license the day after I turned sixteen, and when my parents let me borrow the car, I'd drive around looking for possums and raccoons and garbage cans to run over. I was suspended from high school for fighting. When I was nineteen I broke my right hand on a two-by-four stud behind the sheetrock wall of my studio apartment, and at twenty-one I broke that same hand punching a cocky fat-faced Mexican in the ear. He insulted my sister in a bar and told me to fuck off when I asked him to apologize. I was aiming for his nose but I was drunk.

After we grappled a few seconds he landed a few good punches and split open my left eyebrow. I didn't mind—sharp pain is better than an ache. We bumped into some people and before I knew it there were green plastic chairs and brown bottles and fists and curse words flying around. He got beat pretty badly by two guys I'd never seen before and ended up near unconscious on the floor. His head was propped up against the wall.

"Hey," I said. His eyes fixed on mine. "You should be nicer to people." Then—but only twice—I jumped on his face.

My father picked me up at the police station and we went to The Wharf and didn't speak to each other. I never studied physics but you can fill silence with Bud bottles. I took a sip, wondering what was in his bloodshot blue eyes: disappointment, pride, dust . . . They looked like gasoline rainbows in parking-lot puddles. Torn pieces of my Bud label were all over the mahogany bar. Nervous confetti. I took another sip.

He told me his stories: his fights (two beers), his old girlfriend Babs Zarabinski (one beer), the size of my grandfather's hands (half a beer); how once in a bar he turned to his buddy Georgie Rice and said, "I'd like to bite her on the ass and pray for lockjaw," and how Georgie Rice ran across the bar, slid on his knees, and did it (the other half); how Georgie Rice is dead now (shot of whiskey). He told me about his Harley wreck when he lost his leg (one beer); how he spent a year in the Charleston navy hospital in a full-body cast, how he tried to kill himself with three weeks' worth of pain killers (shot of whiskey). He explained how the brain perceives a missing limb, how sometimes he feels an ache or an itch where there isn't anything, how he can wiggle his missing toes.

My father ordered another two beers and things started blurring together, as if punctuation marks were rationed. Words and time went missing. The two bottles slid an inch after the bartender's hand to a stop in front of us. My father held out a ten-dollar bill but the bartender looked past him and ran to the end of the bar and out. A short guy that reminded me of a Melba Round took a swing at this taller guy

broken glass.

I thought maybe

I was wrong.

a cigarette and

the creases in my father's face.

diagonal lines in denim

black gum on the sidewalk,

mailbox 3

five steps up

door.

doorknob.

I woke up to glass breaking and I heard him mumble. It was 7:03 a.m. I closed my eyes and opened them and it was 7:16. I went to see if he was OK.

"I was hoppin' to the bathroom and the mirra fell off."

"The big one on the door?"

"Yeah."

I made coffee. We drank in silence, except for spoons, a swallow, kitchen's hum. He had work and wanted to get on the road before traffic, so I walked him out to the car. It was raining.

He climbed in, to the *bing . . . bing . . .* of an open door, to the crunch of Styrofoam cups, the crinkle of grease-stained deli brown bags from his bacon, egg, and cheeses. He backed out and pulled away. I watched him till he got around the corner before looking down at where his car had been parked. Raindrops were rippling a puddle of antifreeze.

SUPER MARKETS

I'm a male, you can tell just by looking, I've got sideburns. The sideburns I've got are the kind you can see even if my nose is pointing at you—they've got volume. Also I'm white with brown hair, not white with blond hair or black with black hair, so there's contrast. Plus I was staring at the not-very-green peas in the bow tie pasta salad—maybe they were capers— which was behind the glass counter, which was down and to the left of where I was standing, so I'm sure my right sideburn was in full view from the deli clerk's line of sight. When she finally looked up from washing a shiny metal mixing bowl and saw me there waiting to order my favorite sandwich—the Tuscany, it's Italian—she turned off the faucet and yelled, "Vaness! Vanessa! Come out front and help this lady!" Initially I thought she was referring to someone else, but she wasn't, I checked both shoulders. Then I just kind of left.

On the way home I made the mistake of answering the phone when my sister called, and then the mistake of telling her what had just happened to me. She laughed so hard she had a coughing fit, then brought up the time we were at the ShopRite together because Sparkles needed new dog food because our parents had been feeding her some cheeseburger-flavored stuff that had made her so fat when she sat down her back legs disappeared under a roll of blubber. We were in line to pay for the quality diet stuff when this lady approached me and said, "S'cuse me, hi, I just needed to ask you . . . are you related to Nance Panetieri over on Biltmore? The resemblance is just, oh my gawd"—and here she rolled her fingers in front of my face like she'd just performed a magic trick on my nose—"it's as*tawn*ishing." Then she exhaled for effect and made her eyes big at me while she waited for my response, which was no, I'm not. After my sister finished out-loud-remembering that, I told her that she was not nice and probably a dyke, and she said at least I don't look like one and hung up.

Even though it was a couple extra miles from my apartment I started shopping at a different supermarket, a Pathmark, which was a little pricier but seemed cleaner and had better lighting. Things went pretty well there for a while until I found myself next to the soups one night. I took a step back and looked up the soups and down the soups and up at the fluorescent lights and the ceiling, and then I spun in a circle and realized I was basically in a warehouse full of food and felt completely overwhelmed. A similar thing happens to me in libraries and while looking at the menus of certain Greek diners on Long Island. There are just too many choices to choose from, so nothing stands out, and before I know it the waitress is coming back again and I still don't know what I want because I've been wondering about bison and commercial freezers or something and can't make a decision so I say nothing, thanks, I'm sorry, and go sit in my car and deep breathe and squeeze the steering wheel.

So, there I was, thinking I gotta get the fuck outta here right now, and headed with haste for the exit. I was halfway across the parking lot listening to the change jingle in my left pocket when I heard, "Hey! You! You gonna pay for that candy bar?!"

I spun and saw a blond guy in a blue vest coming straight for me. And when adults are blond and guys—adult blond guys—I for some reason have a difficult time being not-bothered by them. Blond women don't bother me, and neither do blond children. But nine out of ten adult blond males do bother me, because I think they should have grown out of it already. So when I saw him there, something inside my chest sunk, and I pointed at it with an index finger.

"Me?"

"*Yeah. You.* You like to steal candy bars?"

"No," I said. "I don't."

"Then why'd you steal that candy bar?"

"I didn't steal a candy bar."

"Well then why did one of my employees just tell me they saw you steal a candy bar?"

I best-guessed it was because they were old and maybe had poor vision. This must have made some sense to him because he stood blinking at me for a few seconds while he considered it. Then he said, "I don't think so, son."

"Son? I'm thirty."

"Really? You look younger than that."

"Thanks."

At this point a black car that looked like a Toyota Camry to me—but most cars look like Toyota Camrys to me—made its slow way up the row of parked Toyota Camry–looking cars toward us, and we both glanced at it.

"Let me see what's in your pockets," he said, every now and again glancing at the slow-moving car.

"Sure," I said, glancing at the slow-moving car. Then we both just stared at it, and after what seemed like a really long time, and actually may have been a really long time, the car finally arrived to where we were standing and rolled to a stop. The passenger-side window slid down, and the blond-haired blue-vested guy and I both stooped to see inside it, where a not-unattractive lady with her brown hair done up in an up-top bun leaned over and said, "Hi."

"Hey," I said.

"Evening, ma'am," the blond guy said.

"Could either of you tell me where the Blue Legume is?" the lady asked.

"Sure," said the blond guy. "I *love* that place. If you haven't been before, I recommend the miso kelp noodles with tempeh and shitake mushrooms."

"Ooooh," she said. "That sounds delicious."

"No it doesn't," I said.

"It's really amazing," the blond guy said. "But whatever you order, ask for a side of the brazil nut Parmesan. Trust me." He then proceeded to give her very thorough directions before the woman thanked him and rolled up her window, then made her slow way to the parking-lot exit, put on her left blinker, stayed there for what seemed like a really long time even though there were no cars coming, and made a right turn.

I emptied my pockets. In the front left was change, in the front right were dollar bills, in the back right was my wallet, and in the back left was the 3 Musketeers I'd stolen. I handed it to him and he told me never to come back, and I said I was sorry and assured him I wouldn't.

Over the course of the next few months I drifted between supermarkets and just regular markets and organic co-op markets and corner stores, during which all of the following occurred:

- Having just parked, I was heading toward the entrance of a Waldbaums when a white plastic bag floated up and out of an abandoned and otherwise empty shopping cart. Without breaking stride or changing pace or altering my gait in the slightest, I and the bag intersected one another, two vectors converging on the same point at the same time, as if it had been planned and executed perfectly. I had to do no more than hold up my left hand, the bag floated into it, and I continued on my way into the supermarket, where I deposited it in a conveniently located box labeled SHOPPING BAG RECYCLING CONTAINER.

- As I was sitting on a curb eating a rice ball outside of an organic grocery store/co-op place, a guy with too many accessories on walked up and asked me if I had any change. I said, "Dude, I'm eating a rice ball." He said, "OK, can I sit down?" "Do whatever you want," I said, wanting him to change his mind about wanting to sit down. He sat down and asked me where I was from. "Oakdale," I said, "a shithole on the south shore," then took another bite of my rice ball. After chewing and swallowing and taking closer inventory of his hat and bandana and piercings and neckerchief and jewelry and odor, the silence grew long enough to bother me, so I gave in and asked him where he was from. He said, "Nowhere." I said, "All right then, where were you born?" He said, "On a plane," got up, and walked away.

• Someone—I don't know who—ate half an apple, then tried to hide it under a bag of baking chocolate.

• In the shopping cart in front of me in the checkout line was a baby, and it was staring at me and showing me its gums, so I made a face and baby-waved at it. It giggled, so I made a face and baby-waved at it some more, and the mother looked at me and smiled, and I smiled at her like: *Don't worry, I won't kill it or anything. I'm nice.* The baby continued smiling its gums at me, and I didn't know what to do next, I don't have any other baby interaction moves besides making faces and waving, but I felt like I should do something, so I said, "Hey baby. Come here often?" Then I winked and pointed at it and made a clicking noise. The baby stopped smiling and tilted its head to the side like a dog, and then I noticed the mother staring at me in a way that made me feel really self-conscious, so I pretended I'd forgotten Hot Pockets and stepped out of line.

- Overweight Woman #1: "Oh my god . . . who the hell would spend seven dollars on a bag of candy?"
Overweight Woman #2: "How big is the bag?"

- A little Mexican girl, five or six years old, was crying near the orange juices. Seeing no one else around I figured she'd wandered away from her parents, maybe, or they'd wandered away from her. Either way I watched for a while, considering what to do, decided it would be too weird if I approached her, so I didn't do anything except get cereal.

- I signed a shitload of petitions outside of a Whole Foods, more than I can remember, and I can remember war, torture, genocide, his and her's cancer, regular cancer, gay rights, women's rights, prisoners' rights, veterans' rights, AIDS, Guantanamo is bad, stem cell research, a homeless shelter for children, autism, New Orleans, education, drinking water, and one black kid who needed money to get to a track meet in Kansas. I gave what I could.

- Announced over the PA system of a Trader Joe's: "Jennifer, the bananas are here."

Eventually I grew tired of roaming and one day, in a pinch, I returned to shopping at the King Kullen where the deli clerk had mistaken me for female. I grabbed what I needed and found myself in line reading *TIME*'s issue of the one hundred most influential people while I waited for a lady to finish paying for a jar of Ragu. She was having a difficult time with the Verifone debit/credit card thing, and apologized to me for the delay. I waved my hand dismissively. "It's fine," I said, "no rush," and returned to reading about a Korean pop star named Rain who apparently has a killer bod and good moves, and wears vests, and is influential. When I finished with that I turned the page and found this: "Some handsome men are like diamond bracelets." I spun that sentence around in my brain, considering it from all angles, and gave up trying to figure it out almost immediately. Instead I closed the magazine, and gently placed it back on the magazine rack while the register lady rang up my items.

My items: cat food, applesauce, TUMS smooth dissolve tablets, and eggs.

The total was six- or seventeen dollars and change. I didn't have any cash, and the credit card I had planned to use was not in my wallet. I panicked a little, checked all four pants pockets—front right, front left, back right, back left—poked through my wallet again, then tried another card that I knew wouldn't work, twice. Ellie, according to her name tag, folded her arms at me. Not knowing how to behave, I exaggerated my bewilderment, and explained that it was very strange, very strange, because I was quite sure that I had money in that account. "It doesn't make any sense," I said convincingly. Then I shrugged at my shoes and started toward the door.

I'd made it only a few steps when Ellie said, "If that's the case then why don't you try the ATM there," and then she pointed to the ATM there, which stood next to the gumball machines that sell silvery stickers that say BABYGIRL and shit like that. I coughed, and it tasted like iron.

Why Ellie didn't just let me walk out the door and off the hook, I don't know. Maybe she believed me, but I don't think so. I think what she really wanted to know was if I actually believed myself, and I didn't. I walked to the ATM anyway, not hoping for anything at all.

There, I inserted my card, chose English, and entered my PIN, 9-7-7-6, which spells YRPN, which is short for YOUR PIN. After verifying to myself and that little round camera that yes, I had no money in any of my accounts, I stared at a gumball machine that sold enchanted charm bracelets, and then I looked over my shoulder. Ellie was still watching me, waiting. I smiled a fake smile at her, and she smiled a fake smile back, and I started digging through my wallet again, hoping to find that credit card, instead finding a receipt from Ben Franklin— a shitty arts and crafts store I used to go to with my mother— for some stuff I couldn't remember buying. I was wondering about that when a very large security guard guy walked over and stood next to me, his big back against the big shelf of charcoal and lighter fluid and fake logs.

He looked Eastern European—stupid, white, and durable— and he hung his big hands on his belt by his thumbs and stared straight ahead. I turned to see what he was staring at, and my best guess was the endcap of Pasta Roni. I resumed my wallet search, and had just found a dirty toothpick when he said, "Done with ATM?" and I said, "Guess so. Why?" and he said,

"I need to use." "Oh," I said, stepping aside, "sorry," just then realizing that I had left the credit card I was looking for on my desk after buying a falcon glove online in the middle of a sleepless-despite-the-pills kinda night. Then the security guard goes, "Further away, please." And when I look at him, he's looking at me, and he's reaching for his handgun, then drawing his handgun, then pointing it at my feet, then my legs, then my chest, then gesturing for me to move with it. I turned to look for something, maybe someone, anyone, I don't know, and what I saw were rows of people lined up to buy items like cheese and shampoo and cookies and juice. And in the middle of it all was Ellie, still watching me, her eyebrows raised halfway up her forehead in alarm, the look on her face completely void of any sense of inevitability, as if countless variations of this haven't happened countless times before.

Their Appointed Rounds

Outside, in the gravel and weed parking lot, near a log that means *Don't go any further or you'll drive into the bay*, I said, "Donny, Donny, Donny wake up. Wake up, Donny. Donny, wake up. Donny, Donny, Donny, you're a mailman . . ." And then I kicked him, gently, in the ribs. He did not wake up.

I'd seen him earlier, sitting at the bar, craning his neck down to his drink, droopy-eyed, and then I didn't see him, and then I did again as I was walking into the men's room. He was walking out, wiping his chin with his shiny shirtsleeve, just after he had vomited in the sink and on the sink and on the floor, and some of the raviolis were still whole like he hadn't chewed them. I had no words for it at the time, just looked at the mess and dismissed it with a kind of lazy resentment, then headed into the stall farthest from the smell. After peeing a piece of toilet paper around the bowl I flushed with my left foot, and when I returned to my place at the bar, Donny was gone.

I spent the next couple hours watching my twenties turn into a messy pile of fives and tens and singles and quarters. I also nodded, occasionally, at a guy whose head looked like it was made of porcelain, as he told me about the latest argument he had with his girlfriend. His account of it was that they had taken the train into the city and were planning to go to the Bronx Zoo because she likes orangutans. Before they got there, though, they stopped at a pizzeria. She ordered a slice of regular pizza, but he ordered a beef patty, which I've never had but according to him is a pastry-thing stuffed with spiced beef. He told me that it's Jamaican and delicious, and that he wanted her to try it, but she didn't want to try it. He told her, C'mon, just try it, just take a bite. But she said No thanks, so he asked Why not, and she said I don't want to. He said he didn't understand, just try it, and she said No, really, I don't want it. It became a thing for him, and then he pleaded with her to try it, like No, seriously, you have to try this, just take a bite, you have to. But she refused to try it, so then he told her that if she didn't try it he wasn't going to the fucking zoo, and she started crying. Of course he felt terrible about her crying at first, then he just didn't anymore. But still, he apologized, over and over, but she was very upset and wouldn't stop crying, so he leaned in closer and quietly pleaded with her to stop crying, Please stop crying, people are watching. She blurted out, *I don't care if people are watching!* And, not knowing what else to do, he just watched her cry for a while, then looked down at her half-eaten slice of regular pizza, thought it looked a little greasy and was struck by how small her bite mark was, and for some reason this excited him and he felt his dick tingle a little, but then he called her a fucking

moron and brought up the time she said she didn't like guacamole because it was too spicy.

At this point he stopped and looked right at me, which he
hadn't done before, and asked, "Am I wrong about this? I
mean, is guacamole spicy?" I considered it, then answered that
guacamole, done correctly, is not spicy, I don't think. He was
so pleased at having this suspicion confirmed that he bought
my next drink. Eventually he wasn't next to me anymore. I
don't know where he went.

Not long after that I spotted a woman dressed too elegantly
for the bar we were in, sitting alone at a table with her back to
the unlit fireplace. She looked like she could be anywhere from
her late twenties to early forties, and in the middle of my inven-
torying her fanciness an overweight guy in boat shoes with an
unlit cigar in his mouth walked over and joined her. They were
obviously married, and I watched them talk quietly about I
don't know what, and I don't know what it was about them
but I continued studying them for some time before it occurred
to me that they probably had children, probably two children.
Then I imagined their two children for a while, their names and
ages, all the way down to their OshKosh B'gosh overalls, and
I meant it, no joke, when I hoped that they were having a fun
time with their babysitter. That is when I knew I'd had too
much to drink and should leave immediately.

But I didn't leave immediately. First, I stared at the couple
until they stared back and, maintaining eye contact the entire
time, I jammed a handful of bar nuts into my mouth, chewed
them with verve, and swallowed. Then, like a sick boy showing Mommy that yes, I swallowed the medicine, I opened my
mouth as wide as possible and stuck my tongue out—*See? All*

gone!—smirked and raised my eyebrows like, your move, assholes. Then I left.

I hadn't thought about Donny again at all until I was headed to my car and saw him lying there, on his stomach, by the log. At first I didn't know what it was, and when I figured that out I didn't know who. I crept up on him the same way I do when I come across a wild rabbit, and then I just stood there, staring at his hair. Eventually I determined that he was breathing.

I didn't know what to do, and I thought about leaving him there. We hadn't been friends since elementary school, ever since he punched me in the side of the head during a math test for no apparent reason. He's actually remembered as the kid who punched people for no apparent reason, and also as the kid who always fucked up the Maypole dance. After he hit me we didn't really communicate again until the eleventh grade, and then it was mostly by tilting our chins at each other and exchanging heys. When we'd see each other at the bar we'd tilt our chins, exchange heys. Sometimes, if I happened to be outside when he was delivering the mail, I'd wave.

I kicked him harder the second time, and without looking he felt around with his left hand, discovered my right shoe, patted around the laces, and untied the knot. I found it strangely endearing, his refusal to behave in spite of his vulnerability.

"Let me drive you home," I said.

He rolled onto his back and squinted at me, looked a little like Joe Cocker having a fit on stage. "No."

"Donny. You need to get your mailman rest in your mailman bed."

"You're a raging asshole," he said. "A royal son of a bitch."

"Maybe," I said, and looked out over the bay and watched

the moonlight do its shiny thing on the water. Then I sat on the log and lit a cigarette and considered my options. After a few drags I patted him on the shoulder. "Let me give you a ride home, Donny," I said. "Let me help you out."

"Fine," he said.

I grabbed his arm with my left hand and his armpit with my right and helped him up and over and into my beat-up Camry, a hand-me-down from my mother that I'd hated for years. After she died I just half-hated it. The radio only picked up WBAB, an easy-listening station that she always liked but I didn't, and when I turned it on a man was singing something awful about love so I turned it off.

We drove in silence for a while, and just after crossing the Snapper Inn Bridge he started dry heaving so I signaled and pulled over. He had some trouble with the seat belt and then with the door handle, but eventually he managed both and fell out of the car, then crawled toward the little bit of salt marsh that remained after the giant houses with sump pumps in always-wet basements got built. I stepped out and leaned on the hood, and a streetlight humming a little bit down the road shut off. Sometimes I think they do that just for me—shut off when I approach.

I looked up at the stars while Donny retched and spit, inhaled and spit, on and on until he stopped. Then he started again, and I listened again, and when it seemed like he was finished I walked over and asked him if he was all right. "I'm great," he said. "Real good." Then the streetlamp clicked once and hummed back on and I saw orange-colored strings of vomit dangling from his mouth and his nostrils. I pointed to the cattails at first, then let my hand drop to what looked like it might be poison ivy and told him to wipe his face with the leaves. He wiped with his shiny shirtsleeve.

"Should've used the cattails," I said.

"Cattails?"

"You know," I said. "The pussy willows."

He told me that he was terrified of his brother.

"He'll be waiting up for me, man. Once, when I came in around this time, he head-butted me and broke my nose. He's really strong. He's only thirteen, but he's like a man already."

"Everybody's scared of something."

I turned and walked around the car and climbed back in, started it up, looked at him standing there swaying in the just-a-little breeze, looked past him at the cattails swaying in the just-a-little breeze, rolled down the passenger-side window with the driver's-side button.

"You gonna get in?"

"No."

"Get in," I said.

"No."

"Get in the fucking car, Donny."

He said no a third time and started hissing at me like a swan, or cat, or moron. I told him to quit hissing but he kept at it for a while, then got in the car and refused to wear his seat belt. I said, OK, whatever you like, then signaled and pulled onto the road. As I was getting up to speed he leaned forward and turned the radio on. Another man was singing something awful about love, and—as I reached to shut it off—Donny punched me right in the temple. My head bounced off the driver's-side window and everything whited out, like an overhead projector had been turned on inside my skull. I felt myself slouch forward and my left hand loosen on the steering wheel, my right foot ease off the gas. I heard possible and impossible things: the car engine winding down, the tires humming lower on the road, Donny breathing, my breathing, grass breathing, crickets cricketing in the night like *I'm-a-cricket, I'm-a-cricket . . . I'm-a-cricket-too . . .* cattails and pussy willows swaying in the just-a-little breeze. I heard my mother's voice say my name, just once, but it hung there, suspended in the ether around me before fading out. Then I heard and thought and felt nothing at all, just black and quiet, like before you're born.

Sometime later, like *blip*, I came back on. I knew before I opened my eyes that I was in the passenger seat of my car, that my car was parked in front my house, and that it was Donny's hand on my shoulder, gently shaking me, him saying, "Wake up, Alby. Alby. Alby. Alby, wake up."

REST STOP

I stuck around a few months after my brother and sister abandoned ship—supposedly to keep an eye on him but really because I couldn't do much of anything except sit around wondering what my mother's body looked like rotting in an expensive box under the ground; also 'cause he had a big TV—and one Sunday morning I came downstairs to find him at the kitchen table staring at a crossword puzzle through lopsided, one-armed reading glasses on the end of his nose. In front of him were six or seven crushed-up Bud cans, one un-crushed, a bag of oatmeal cookies, and he had a giant scab down the left side of his face, and parts of it were still bleeding.

"Good morning, Dad," I said, filling up the kettle.

"Morning," he said.

The stove clicked three times before flaming, same as always, and I went and got a coffee cup out of the coffee cup cabinet and leaned against the counter.

"King of bread," he said. "Three letters. Third is *e*."

I thought about bread for a while.

"I don't know," I said, because I didn't, then walked over and looked at the crossword over his shoulder, then at his still-bleeding face some more, then at the crossword some more. "No idea."

I turned around and stared out the window at two squirrels hanging off a wooden bird feeder. There was no seed in the feeder, hadn't been any for years. They were chewing on the wood roof.

"We should get some birdseed," I said. "For the squirrels."

"Tijuana Brass trumpeter Herb. Six letters. Fourth is *e*."

"You could misspell parsley," I said. "Add a couple *e*'s to weed. *Weeeed*."

"He's not a fuckin' plant," he said. "He's a musician. His first name is Herb."

"Avore. Herb Avore."

He shook his head. "Stupid."

When the water started boiling I poured it into my coffee cup, added a tea bag, watched the brown billow and went to the fridge for half-and-half.

"Mae and Nathaniel, five letters."

"Wests," I said. "What happened to your face?"

"I fell off my bike."

It made sense as far as explanations go. This was summer, festival season on Long Island—Lobsterfest, Clamfest, Oysterfest, some Indian powwow thing, and an antique boat show—and in order to avoid driving drunk he had taken to riding my sister's bike to some of these, drinking till he was asked or made to leave, then trying to pedal home.

"That your breakfast?"

He flashed me some kind of look and stuffed a whole cookie into his mouth and began chewing it in what I think was supposed to be an aggressive manner. He resembled a giant, unhappy five year old, and it unsettled me.

"I tried to eat a hard-boiled egg," he said, "but the shell wouldn't come off easy."

"Want me to get you somethin' from the deli?"

"No," he said to a spot on the floor near my feet.

"Thinkin' about mopping?"

"No."

"Jealous I have ten toes?"

"No."

"Are you smart?"

He stuffed another cookie in his mouth and stood up and stalked off to finish his crossword in front of the big television. I gave the back of his head the middle finger, rinsed a few dishes in the sink, and placed them in the dishwasher. Then I raided his pills. He'd somehow managed to convince an idiot at the VA that he had ADHD, when really he was just depressed after the chemo killed my mother, which for some reason I imagine is like little tiny nuclear bombs going off inside you till you're dead and then some. Maybe moths can hear the explosions.

To be fair, the Ritalin did help him get out of bed and through his day, but the way me and my siblings saw it, side effects included anxiety, irritability, patriotism, one night in the Sayville Modern Diner he asked, "What's broccoli?" and another night he ate two Beef Merlot Lean Cuisines and a loaf of pumpernickel bread, then threatened to commit suicide with the butter knife. My brother had, the week before, returned to graduate school, so it was left to me to wrestle the butter knife from him, and we fell to the kitchen floor and knocked over Sparkles's water dish and rolled around in the puddle for a while, which had swollen-up dog-food crumbs in it and smelled. After she got bored with watching from the doorway, my sister walked over and yanked his artificial leg off and ran out of the house with it. This stunned him, and he quit struggling long enough for me to make a proposal:

"Stop being an asshole."

"No."

I thought about that, then counterproposed to get his leg for him if he promised not to try to kill himself again. He thought about that, then agreed and added, "Now get the fuck off me."

"Promise first."

"I fuckin' promise!"

"You fuckin' promise what?"

"I fuckin' promise not to try to kill myself!"

"Good!" I said. "It fuckin' pleases me to hear you say that, Dad!"

Then I rolled off him onto my back, and together the two of us lay there in the puddle staring up at the dead bug silhouettes in the fluorescent lights trying to catch our breath. Eventually I hit him lightly on the chest with the back of my open hand. Eventually he reached across himself and shook it.

The batteries in the orange flashlight were dead, so I went to the battery drawer and spent a minute putting in and taking out dead batteries. Eventually I found a combination that worked, but barely, and as soon as I got outside the light went dim and died, so I shook it a little before throwing it at a tree. When it hit the trunk it flashed bright for half a second, then fell to the ground where I left it. Then I walked a lap around the outside of the house in the dark.

Halfway into lap two I spotted my sister across the street at the end of the dock, staring down into the brown water of the Connetquot River, while I walked out to the end of the dock and stood next to her and didn't say anything, just stared down into the brown water of the Connetquot River. She didn't say anything either. I patted my pockets and found my cigarettes, patted them again and found my lighter, lit two and handed her one. Neither of us said anything. We just smoked and stared down into the brown water of the Connetquot River, while I wondered if turtles can get hepatitis. Clams can—Isabella Rossellini did a PSA-thing about it once, I saw the billboard for it on the westbound platform of the Babylon train station. Standing there on the end of the dock with my sister I suddenly felt very tired.

"Where is it?" I said.

"I threw it in the bushes," she said, then turned and pointed.

I followed the tip of her finger out with my eyes and, squinting, was just able to make out a foot with a black sneaker on it protruding from the top of one of the shrubs bordering the property.

The two of us turned and stared down into the water again, and after what seemed like a long time, I crushed my cigarette out on the bottom of an upside-down bucket placed over one of the rotting pilings of the dock and said, "Poor turtles," but more mumbled than pronounced, like, "Prtrtles." Then I patted my sister's shoulder awkwardly, retrieved the leg out of the bush, and headed into the house with it under my arm like a gift.

My father was at the kitchen table reading a days-old newspaper, stuffing handfuls of croutons into his face. When he saw me he wiped his left hand down his denim shirt twice, then reached out for the leg like, *Gimme*. I handed it to him, and he immediately started picking small branches and bits of shrub out of the stump socket and dropping them on the floor, then turned the whole thing upside down and shook it. When satisfied, he placed the leg on the floor in front of him, rolled up his pants leg to just above the knee, pushed his stump into the stump socket with both hands, then stood up and shifted his weight from right to left to right again, like a junior high school dancer. Then he bent down and pulled the neoprene stump sleeve up over the knee, rolled his pants leg down, sat back in the chair, and resumed reading the days-old newspaper. I told him I was going to bed.

He turned to look at the stove clock. "It's only eight thirty," he said.

I didn't answer him, just wiped a piece of swollen-up dog food off his shoulder and went upstairs to my room and fell asleep and didn't get up till three the next day. My sister was packing.

A festival or two later I came home around ten or eleven to find a running pickup truck in front of the house, the taillights tinting the exhaust red, tinting the bushes and the mailbox red, the guy struggling to unload my sister's bicycle from the back of the truck red. I parked and hurried over to help, and as I got closer I saw that my father was also in the back of the truck, on his back, tugging at the front wheel. When he noticed me there he yelled, "Hey kid!" then just lay there smiling and blinking, like he was genuinely happy to see me.

"Hey Dad," I said. That's all it took. Something in my voice must have betrayed some sense of disappointment, or concern, or just wasn't enthusiastic enough, because the smile slowly came off his face and his eyes went vague and unfocused, as if he just at that moment remembered something unpleasant. He turned and looked out over the lawn.

"You gotta leave me here," he said. "Just fuckin' leave me here."

A week later, I did.

I'd probably eaten four or five Ritalin and snorted another off a paperback with a rolled-up oil-change receipt, plus I'd downed a lukewarm cup of burnt gas station coffee a few miles back, so my heart felt like it might bust right out of my chest and float there over the steering wheel all shiny-style like Jesus's or Mary's or Whoever's that was by the time I pulled into the rest stop—one of those generic-looking ones, a sand-colored single-story with the men's room on one side and the women's on the other, the vending machines in the middle, a picnic table or two off to the right. I had to go so bad I power-walked up the path and was unzipped and dick out five feet from the men's-room door. Once inside I saw that both urinals were stopped up with paper towels so I hobbled then hopped into the first of two stalls and saw what looked like a murder scene only browner and with spinach. I hopped into the handicapped stall and fired at will, shuffled my way closer and was peeing and staring at the ceiling and then at the wall and then at the toilet and then at the floor and then at a grasshopper on the floor to the right. At first I'd just given the grasshopper a quick look, but then I gave it another because it seemed, in its absolute stillness, to be staring at me.

I thought of a painting in the hallway outside my brother's and my childhood bedroom of two cartoonish kids with oversized heads and big eyes that, whenever I worked up the courage to look at them, seemed to be looking at me. The grasshopper's effect was similar. I didn't like it.

I continued staring back at the grasshopper, and it continued staring at me, like in a staring contest or showdown, and after a while I said to it, "Shoo, dude." But it didn't shoo, and it didn't "scram" or "get the fuck outta here" either—it just stared. Finally I stomped my right foot at it and it catapulted itself directly into the toilet bowl, where it began paddling around at panicked random, circles and Xs, ovals and figure eights.

My one experience with near-drowning is that it's uncomfortable. Also, I lifeguarded at a small inground pool at a home for mentally disabled people back in the early nineties, and there was a guy there named Joe Pepe who liked vacuum cleaners so much that all the nurse's aides cut vacuum cleaner ads out of the paper and gave them to him as a reward for behaving himself, one of the many things he had no talent for. I once saw him sneak up behind a fellow patient and try to strangle him with a piece of yarn. I don't remember too much else about him except that he looked exactly how a person with Down syndrome and glasses looks like, and that every day, as soon as I showed up for work, he'd tell me he fucked my mom. I'd tell him that he didn't, and he'd tell me that yeah, he did, last night, she loved it, and I'd insist that he didn't, and he'd insist that he did so, and so on. This would continue until I grew tired of the argument and quit, after which he'd make some kind of celebratory noise, then jump and spin and stag-leap his way out of the room. Ballet, but graceless.

What Joe Pepe didn't do though, not ever, at least not while I worked there, was go in the pool. So one day after he started in with the mom stuff I said to him, "I'm sure she enjoyed it, Joe. Why don't you come swim in the pool and we'll talk about it." His face scrunched up. "Awww, what's the matter, Joe," I said. "You're not scared to come into the pool, are you, Joe?" He clenched his fists and spun around two times. "Not you, Joe," I said. "No way. That couldn't be the case, because my mom wouldn't fuck anybody that's scared to go in the pool. She told me so on my thirteenth birthday. She said, 'Happy birthday, Alby, here's your present. It's a card, and in it you'll find five dollars for every year of your life, for a total of *fffffffffffffffff*— sixty-five dollars. I love you very much, and I am very proud of you. You are growing up so fast now, and I just want you to know that I will never fuck anyone who can't swim. Not ever. It's unattractive, and probly means they're a fuckin' moron.' So, Joe, if you really want me to believe that you fucked my mom last night, you're gonna have to prove to me that you can swim. You up for it?"

He sniffled, then wiped his nose then his eye with his wrist. "No!" he yelled. "No no no no no no!"

"Well why not, Joe?"

"I don't wanna," he said.

"Well why don't you wanna?"

" 'Cause I almost drownded once," he said. "It hurt!"

I pissed around the grasshopper as best I could and pinched off as soon as possible. Then I stood there, over it, watching it struggle up the side of the bowl, slip back in and rest. Over and over: Struggle, slip, rest. Struggle, slip, rest. Struggle.

I looked around a little for something to fish him out with and, finding nothing, I simply reached in and scooped him up with my right hand and carried him outside, where I put him on the ground near a bush and nudged him with my index finger. Then—and I may have imagined this but I don't think so—he kinda shook himself dry, like a dog, and jumped one small time. I nudged him again till he made a bigger jump.

Afterward, as I was washing my hands, I guessed that it must've been confused, that I'd startled it, that it had made a mistake. But then I considered the possibility. Of course, I don't really believe an insect has the mental capacity to suffer the kind of anguish one has to in order to *want* to kill oneself, but certainly there's nothing too unreasonable in wondering if things could be so bad for a grasshopper. Two steps toward the paper towel dispenser and I was pretty sure the answer to that question, no matter the animal, is yes.

TESTY

I

Walking wasn't easy with fat legs and a big head; I was three years old and did the best I could. I made it into the kitchen and there, on the floor, was a little baby in a little baby carrier, and my mother's feet were there, and another woman's feet, too. There were often new moms' feet around because mine was a Lamaze instructor and her students liked to come back and show off what came out of them. I waddled over and started petting the little baby on its fat little baby arm, and my mother praised me for making nice. The baby also seemed to enjoy my making nice to it—it cooed and gurgled and showed me its gums—and I continued petting it until my mother and this woman went back to their conversation above me, at the table. Then I started pinching the baby. It got quiet and screwed its face a little. I pinched harder, and when I was most success-ful its head started to shake in a way that seemed involuntary.

Not that much about babies is voluntary, so maybe it'd be better to say that the head shake had something to do with the pain I succeeded in causing it. I dug my nails in—thumb and index—put marks all over its arms and legs like ( ). Still, the baby did not cry. I can't know what I would have done if I were stronger or if I were alone with it, but as it was I just dug my nails in deeper, pinched harder, twisted further, and then finally this baby opened its toothless mouth and let out a whimper, then a wail, and I was proud.

1. **The author's attitude toward babies is one of**
A) objective indifference.
B) violent anger.
C) strong disapproval.
D) qualified regret.

2. **The author suggests that traditional views of human morality are flawed because they**
A) do not allow for differences in age and gender.
B) do not account for change in an individual.
C) fail to arrive at definitive answers.
D) are depressing.

3. **With which of the following statements would the author be most likely to agree?**
A) Women are great.
B) Women's feet are great.
C) Women are often proud of things they shouldn't be proud of.
D) Politeness is a part of good behavior.
E) It depends.

II

There was a traveling animal show in the middle of the Sun
Vet Mall. One part was a chicken-wire petting zoo with goats
and piglets and hay—I liked the piglets—another was a pony
ride, which, according to the black marker written on a white
paper plate and scotch-taped to the fence, cost five tickets. The
man standing at the gate verified that: "Five tickets." My mother
poked around in her coat pockets and pulled out a used tea
bag from the one on the right—my brother and myself and the
man didn't know what to make of that—then put it back in
her pocket and pulled her lady wallet out of the left one. She
snapped it open and took out a five-dollar bill, then four singles,
the three of us watching her pushing coins and cards and receipts
around with her index finger, digging now, and then *Wah-lah!*
she said, pulling out another single. I looked at my brother and
nodded.

She stood there tidying the six bills, the fiver either on the
very bottom or the very top, uncrinkling them with a game of
tug-of-war that her right hand always lost. Then, like it had
only just occurred to her, which it might have but I don't think
so, she asked the man if she could skip the ticket thing and
just pay him the ten dollars in cash. He said no, he needed the
tickets. I was nervous then about what my mother's reaction
would be, but she said OK, and we walked over to the ticket
table, a tiny square with a tiny lady sitting behind it. My mother
smiled and handed her the ten dollars cash, and the little lady
sitting behind it tore ten tickets off the red roll, all of them still
connected like paper sausages. My mother took them and said
thank-you, counted and tore, handed my brother and me each

a string of five. As we walked back toward the gate and the man beside it, I looked at my half of the red tickets, and each of them had TICKET printed on it and a number. I was excited.

My brother went first, and he sat on the pony while it walked. And then it was my turn, and I sat on the pony while it walked. Afterward, we agreed that it was the best thing we'd ever done, and my mom said, *Woo!* and clapped as we headed in the direction of a small crowd.

Curious what they were crowding around, we squeezed through to the front, where there was a tiger lying there not moving except to breathe and occasionally lick the metal bars of its otherwise red cage. It was emaciated and missing patches of hair, and if I'm remembering correctly it didn't have any ears, like maybe it had scratched them off. We stood there, in the crowd, all of us fewer than a dozen, all of us staring at it. Just when my mother tugged on my shirtsleeve, meaning it was time to leave, the tiger slowly stood, arched its back in a stretch, and yawned. Everybody seemed to enjoy that, seeing the inside of its mouth, its tongue and its teeth. When it finished yawning, the tiger walked in a slow circle, its shoulder blades pushing up so high with each step I thought they might pop through its back. Then it stopped walking, lifted its tail, and showed everyone its tigery asshole, and from somewhere just below that, shot out piss directly at my brother's gawking face. It smelled like white rice and pine trees, and later he told me it didn't taste as bad as you might think.

4. According to the above depiction, animals in captivity are
A) loving it, man. Life's a party.
B) victims of the paper sausage trade.

C) fortunate to have rewarding careers in the entertainment industry.

D) hydrated.

5. **Tigers are**

A) totally cool.

B) not as cool as cobras.

C) not as cool as cobras before their tiger ears fall off, but after their tiger ears fall off, tigers are number one.

D) lonely.

6. **How are you feeling?**

A) OK

B) Pretty good

C) Not so good

D) Fucked with

E) Lonely

III

One time, after a winter storm, my sister and I were building an igloo together in the backyard when she stopped in the middle of her brick-making duties to regard a very tall pine tree, its branches bent to the ground under the weight of the snow. When I ordered her back to work, she pointed to the tree and told me how magical and amazing it would be to sled down the branches. "It would be so magical and amazing," she said, "so fast, so glamorous." I admitted that the steep slope did look tempting, in fact I'd even thought of it myself, way before she ever did, first. She said that didn't matter, what matters is who *does it* first, no guts no glory and nobody remembers the Santa Maria. Fine, I said, I'll do it, I can do whatever I set my mind to, Mom said so. However, as I set my mind to it, I began to doubt it was even possible, and as I looked at the tree again I wondered out loud if the glory was worth the risk.

The glory is definitely worth the risk, she said, because if you do it you automatically won't be a fagatron anymore. I wasn't a fagatron, but she was though, and after we argued about that she said, if it made me feel any better, she would climb up there with me and personally hand me my red disk sled. I don't know, I said, let me check it out, and she said too late, forget it, and broke into a slow jog in the direction of the tree. I ran after, and she stopped to wait for me.

I climbed all the way up to the tippy-top of the pine tree and popped my head through. From up there I could see over the roof of the garage and the front of the house to the river and down the block to Dowling College, and in the other direction I saw cars the size of my matchboxes creeping along Montauk Highway. I yelled down to her that it was really high and steep, and she assured me it was both—as she climbed up to hand me my sled—but that snow is soft. I wasn't so sure about that but she was very sure about that and she handed me my sled and said, wait till I'm on the ground with a good view. Fine, I said, but hurry up. *Hurry up!* Hurry or I'm not doing it, I swear. I was about to definitely not do it when she came running out from under the tree and was on the ground with a good view, yelling, go ahead, fagatron, do it. I will, I said, hold on a sec, don't rush me, and, adjusting my footing, I held my sled out in front of me with my left hand, took a deep breath, and let go with the right, tottered just a little and *woosh*.

I fell right through and Plinkoed down four or five or ten branches before my fat leg got caught about halfway to the ground. Then I just hung there upside down, arms limp above (or is it below?) my head, fine and glittery snow floating down all around me.

7. **The passage reveals that**
   A) you can't trust water.
   B) you can't trust trees.
   C) you can't trust girls.
   D) you can't trust people.
   E) you can't trust yourself.
   F) you can't trust.
   G) trust often leads to betrayal, which occasionally, if you're lucky, leads to something lovely.

8. **Do you bruise easily?**
   A) Yes
   B) No
   C) Sometimes
   D) It depends
   E) It depends who's hitting me

NO TEST MATERIAL ON THIS PAGE

IV

We were ten and lined up in center field of the Locust Avenue
Little League ballpark practicing our pop flys. When I stepped
forward, the coach, my father, hit it as hard and as high as he
could. I ran a clumsy zigzag all over the outfield, spun here,
stumbled there, got underneath it, jogged in place, danced nervously waiting for it to come down. I squinted and strained
to keep my eyes on it, made last-second adjustments, fidgeted,
followed it down with unflinching concentration right up until
it hit me in the face. I'd forgotten to put my glove up, woke on
my back in the outfield grass on a warm summer afternoon with
a pretty lady holding an orange Creamsicle to my swollen-shut
left eye. I felt peaceful for at least thirty seconds, and for that
I'll love baseball forever. Years later my father admitted to me
that he never wanted to coach, and that he chose his players
based on who had the best-looking mothers.

9. **The passage is most relevant to which of the following areas
   of study?**

   A) history
   B) psychology
   C) medicine
   D) sports
   E) pretty ladies making things worthwhile
   F) genetics

V

I was twelve years old and running counterclockwise laps
around the outside of the house, counting them out as I

crossed the stone path that curved between the front door and the bashed-in metal mailbox with no number, but if there were a number it would've been a three. I was running and I was counting and I was losing count, distracted by the sound of my own breathing, two or more inhales for every exhale: inhale-inhale-exhale, inhale-inhale-inhale-exhale. I had more trouble remembering the first digit of the lap than the second, so if I was off I was off by tens. Eight or eighteen, nineteen or twenty-nine, fifty or forty, or fifty, it didn't matter. The number wasn't the thing, the thing was the thing. Simply, I hadn't thought of any other thing to do that particular morning, and because I had the energy to do it, that's what I did. I ran laps around the outside of the house, and I counted them out as I crossed the stone path.

After crossing the stone path there was lawn. There was nothing special about the lawn except that it was the lawn that came immediately after crossing the stone path. It was the beginning. After the beginning was the driveway, where I made a left turn and ran up and over and past the oil stains that were blacker than the blacktop they were on, then another left down the cement alley between the back of the house and the rotting stockade fence, on the other side of which lived Zion, a Jewish guy who threatened to cut my father's ears off with a chainsaw during an argument about tree branches and rain gutters. Then out of the cement alley and onto the other section of lawn, past the Japanese maple with bamboo wind chimes, the only wind chimes that don't make me think of walking into Ben Franklin with my mother. Around the patio, more lawn, then the stone path and a number that might or might not have followed the one that preceded it. I'd been going for an hour, maybe more, around and around, because I could, and then I tripped headfirst over a rake that I had most likely left out myself. I've never had the kind of patience it takes to put leaves in bags or rakes back in garages. I hit hard and slid a few feet, stopped and opened my eyes. I stood up quickly, embarrassed even though there was no one around to see it, and looked myself over, blinking and marveling at my indestructibility. Then I looked at my right hand. The pinky and ring finger had seemingly exploded, their insides outside. I sucked air through my teeth and took off running again, faster now, left arm swinging, right arm not, my ruined hand up and out in front of me as I went up the stone path and into the house screaming for my mother, screaming, "Mom! Mom! My guts are out!" She was in the kitchen on the telephone and told whoever it was that she'd call them back, hung up, and pulled me by the shirt toward the window for better light. There, she studied my hand for a few seconds, looked closer, said, "It's dog poop," huffed and wiped it off with a paper towel and sent me to the bathroom to wash up. Only then, when I knew that my hand was fine, did I start crying.

10. What's the problem?

A) Mind over matter.

B) I am matter.

C) I matter.

D) I do not matter.

E) Pain is preferable to pleasure.

F) The virtue of overwhelming pain is that it takes your mind off of problems.

VI

The karaoke guy had been calling us "party people" all night and I'd had enough. He was trying to convince a few of us to go sing songs, so I put my face close to his face and said, "You are a fuckface, Fuckface, and I'm not going anywhere." Then I walked out and found myself hanging on to a parking meter watching the time-remaining zeros peekaboo at me while I considered my left eye. It had begun winking wildly, my impaired brain letting me know one or both would have to close, simply because the inside of an eyelid is dark, and dark doesn't move around so much. I clamped it shut and waited for things to settle. When the right eye started to give me problems I switched over and waited for things to settle. I alternated between the two and waited for things to settle. If you wait for things to settle long enough they usually do, and even though I felt steady enough to stand unaided, I held on to the meter anyway as I took a piss on the white minivan parked there. The puddle looked alive as it moved down the gutter.

Tuck and zip and one step back, I stuffed my hands in my pants pockets and pulled them inside out. A few crumpled dollar bills spilled onto the sidewalk and I bent at the waist like girls do, some of them anyway, picked up the dollars, and stood and began uncrumpling them, felt what looked like a piece of licorice stuck to my hand, looked closer and saw little antennas. I said, Hello, slug, I'm gonna name you Cherokee Bob, and then I thought to see if anybody was watching me. Standing against the outside wall of the bar and the birthday party I'd just removed myself from, below and to the left of a Budweiser neon, was a group of three girls with cigarettes in their hands, staring at me. They didn't say anything, and I didn't say anything, and then after that they didn't say anything. I looked at Cherokee Bob tenderly, then placed him down on the sidewalk in a slow and careful way, nudged him with my index finger, and whispered, Run, go on damn it, run for your fuckin' life, and then I looked at the three girls, who were still looking at me, and the one on the left took a drag of her cigarette, and I said, Nobody touches this fuckin' slug, and began backing away from them, never taking my eyes off them, and the one in the middle took a drag of her cigarette, and none of them said anything.

11. Huh?

A) sentimental heart vs. skeptical mind

B) skeptical heart vs. sentimental mind

C) heart

D) heartbroken

E) heartbroken and furious about being heartbroken

F) heartbroken and furious about being heartbroken and blind drunk

G) the slug symbolizes his dick

EXTRA CREDIT!!!

Now, considering everything you've read, here and everywhere, ever, in your whole fuckin' life—and be honest—what's the point?

A) to help

B) to witness

C) to endure

D) to document

E) to attack power

F) to be an enemy of bullshit

G) to give pain meaning

H) to instruct

I) to entertain

J) to find comfort

K) to fuck as many women as possible

L) to save small animals

M) to avoid loneliness

N) to avoid a nine-to-five

O) to make nice

P) everything dies

Q) don't die yet

R) revenge

S) style

T) restraint

U) fame and fortune

V) F and J only

W) the point is always moving

X) the point is what we do in the meantime

Y) there is no point

Z) Mom

TOAST

I once dated this other girl who, when faced with restaurant-toast, would take only one bite of each of her four restaurant-toast halves. She said she didn't want any of the restaurant-toast halves to feel neglected. "You're a very nice girl," I told her. She thanked me, then complained about the ice cubes in her orange juice.

She had this other habit, too, of putting on ChapStick before drinking her coffee. The first time I noticed it was at the zoo near the giraffes after we patronized the Perky Bean cart in the Wild Time Food Court. She told me she does it because she likes the greasy feel of the ChapStick on her lips with the warm coffee going in. She said, "I like it so much that one time I left my coffee on the porch to go get my ChapStick out of my bag, and while I was inside I got a phone call from my mom that lasted for like twenty minutes. When I finally remembered about the coffee, all these ants had drowned themselves in it, but I drank it anyway."

I looked her up and down and up again and then at a trash can, and then at a yellow jacket flying messy figure eights above the trash can. After a while the yellow jacket started hovering over a piece of what I think was chewed-up gum stuck in the ashtray on top of the can, almost landed, then zipped off to someplace else.

"You drank ants," I said.

"I did."

"Did they taste like anything?"

"Yes," she said. "Like coffee."

I nodded at her, then together we turned and sipped our coffees and watched the giraffes chew leaves. Later, we watched an otter jerk off.

We started dating intense-style, talking all the time on the phone and in person about this and that, our regrets and our fears for the future and lawn care and breast-feeding and the wipe-wash feature on cars, but mostly about what we wanted to eat for dinner. The answer was usually, I don't know, what do you wanna eat? And the answer to that was usually, I don't know, what do *you* want to eat? And so on. Eventually she would go *hmmmm*, then list off ethnic groups in the form of questions—Japan*ese?*—and I would get really frustrated and say Let's just go to Joe's.

Joe's was this dump on Cannery Row with mediocre food but there was no freezer in the kitchen so it was always fresh and pretty cheap, and the first time we ate there we heard an old guy say, "Where the fuck am I? Miami? I hate glass bricks."

We liked it immediately. One table was shaped like a row-boat and one an actual picnic bench. The silverware was mismatched, too, the floor painted-over cracked concrete, the baby-blue walls decorated with pictures of boats and big fish, and a framed newspaper article about a WWII submarine hung outside the only bathroom. It quickly became our special place, and we went at least twice a week. We even had a favorite table in the corner, and got to know one of the waitresses, Jessica, pretty well.

Then one morning my girlfriend followed me into the kitchen and watched me pour myself a bowl of granola and milk and scoop a big spoonful of it into my mouth and commented, "Eating granola, huh?" I was so confounded I stopped chewing to look at her, exactly one-half of me wanting to pinch her cheeks, exactly the other half of me wanting to punch her across the room. I stood quietly for a few seconds until the feelings passed, and when they did I resumed eating my granola. Realizing that I wasn't going to bother with a response, she turned her attention to the window and, noticing a cat outside, declared, "Ohhh, look! A cat!" Then a few seconds later, "That cat is *cuuuute*."

That afternoon, after she'd gone home, she called on the phone to ask if I'd done my laundry.

Also, one night, when she was standing still and naked and backlit by the bathroom light, I noticed a kind of white, almost invisible fur all over her body. It bothered me. I never said anything about it cause I didn't want to hurt her feelings, but she had no problem commenting on how my dick is browner than the rest of me. "It's like the dark circles around Indian people's eyes," she said. I pretended I didn't care, but I did, but not as much as I cared about her shoes. She always wore high heels, like even on bike rides always, and to the beach and batting cages always, and to a Super Bowl party we went to once. And believe me, it wasn't so much that she was a half inch taller than me when she wore them, which she thought it was about—it was that I got sick of hearing her clomping around everywhere like a pony. At first I just made little jokes about it, started calling her Trusty and offering her carrots all the time, said things like, "You can lead a lady to water but you can't make her be sneaky." Soon enough, though, I was promising to shoot her if she ever broke her leg. She got upset, and I said, "It'd be real sad, but I'd have no choice. Sorry." Then I pointed my finger at her like a pistol and went *pchoooo*.

One Sunday she took an hour getting ready to go to the dog park, and I told her to giddy-it the fuck up. She gave me the whole *I do this for you!* thing in the car on the way and I said, "Whoa now. Slow down there Seabiscuit. If you're doing it for me lose the fancy fuckin' footwear. It annoys me."

She got real quiet then, looked out the window at passing stuff, said, "You can just drop me off wherever."

"OK," I said. "How about in the La Brea Tar Pits? Be sure to say hi to the woolly mammoths and sabertooths for me, and I'm not even fucking kidding man."

"Don't call me *man*!" she yelled, and when I glanced over I could see that she'd started crying, which is another thing. She could be very dramatic sometimes, but worse, the drama seemed rehearsed, like she learned it from watching too many lady-movies. She'd cry about stuff that wasn't worth crying about, and allow for all these pregnant pauses and deep breathe and whisper-say something dramatic like: *"You're mean."*

Exhale through mouth, close eyes, shake head slowly, clomp away.

She also wrote me notes, dramatic ones declaring dramatic things like: *Miss you!* And, *You really embarrassed me last night . . . I work with her!* And one time, verbatim, I'm not even kidding, this:

> *Risk or regret.*
>
> *That's the phrase associated with thoughts of you.*
>
> *You are someone I invest my time in who is an impossible situation.*
>
> *I think you are amazing.*
>
> *I haven't felt connected to anyone the way I do with you every morning we wake up together.*
>
> *Risk or Regret.*
>
> *Almost every night before I go to bed.*
>
> *Risk or Regret.*

I didn't know what to do with that info so I put a C+ at the top of it and gave it back. More drama. More whisper talk. More clomping.

I felt bad about that one and followed her out of the room and told her I was only kidding and that I was sorry. She said, regular volume, "Sorry for what? Do you even know?" I said for being a jackass. "That's a start," she said. But instead of explaining that I'm a moron and don't wanna fall in love and have to fuck her forever, I just kissed her and fucked her for what felt like forever.

So there were things about each other we grew not to like, and the sex went from three or four positions to one or two, sometimes one or none when one or both of us was tired, which was a lot. We made each other yawn. I got to know the fillings in her back teeth.

We started spending most weeknights on the couch watching *America's Funniest Home Videos* and animal documentaries. We were watching this one where they have slow-motion aerial footage of a wolf chasing a mother and baby gazelle all over Mongolia for like ten minutes, and sometime early on the mother and baby got split up, so then it was just the wolf and the little gazelle, but the little gazelle could really move, I mean, *really* move, so they're zigging and zagging and leaping and then just flat-out *going* until the little gazelle gets tired and collapses to the ground and the wolf eats him up, just fuckin' rips him apart, but then later on we find out the wolf eventually starves to death anyway, and then this baby elephant goes blind in a sandstorm but continues following his mother's footprints using only his sense of smell, only he follows them in the wrong direction so he dies, too, when all of a sudden I felt her scooching closer to me on the couch and I looked at her, and without even turning away from the TV she out of nowhere says she wants to try anal sex. I blinked at her ear for a few seconds before saying, "OK." And before you know it I was Frenching her, and then before you know it I was doing my high school locker combination move on her (33-14-4) followed by my lazyboy technique and then my eating-her-pussy maneuvers before she pulled me up by my hair and rolled on her side and I stuck it in there and moved it around for a while. The whole time she talked her dirty talk, every now and again dropping in half-rhetorical questions to encourage my participation, but it didn't work cause I always gave one-word answers.

". . . you like having your cock in my ass, Mister Bad Boy?"

"Yep."

And it went on like that, not for too long, just right up until she started yelling don't stop. Then, after the ten seconds where I remain perfectly still with my mouth open for some reason, I apologized and went wide-legged into the kitchen for paper towels like a gentleman.

Overall I'd say it was OK—like going through a little door into a big room. I prefer vaginas. But what was a lot of fun though was to pretend that she got pregnant from it, and then the next day to pretend that she gave birth to our turd-baby and that we named him Francis. The day after that she broke up with me by dramatic note, which basically said, I can't do this anymore, which I read and then put in the sink garbage disposal. For the next few nights I dreamt she left me angry voicemails about my laundry, and for the next few weeks I wondered what it meant and back-and-forthed about trying to win her back, exactly one-half of me wanting to, exactly the other half of me not. I decided nothing, and realized I suck at making decisions. My younger brother, on the other hand, doesn't. He slept with three women, decided he liked the third, and married her. This is despite our on-her-deathbed-in-the-den mother saying, "AJ, you know I love Tara, but don't you think you should have some fun first?" He squeezed her hand and told her his mind was made up. I set about the business of unmaking it five minutes later, in the kitchen, by demanding he honor our mother by fucking more girls. He looked me right in the hairdo and said, "Sorry bro."

"Don't apologize to me," I said. "Apologize to that woman in there, because you're breaking her fucking heart. Then apologize to yourself when your marriage falls apart in ten years but now you're balder and fatter and can't get the quality ass you can right now. Then reject the apology 'cause you don't deserve forgiveness, you divorced piece a shit!"

"You're a moron piece a shit," he said.

"I don't think so."

"I know so."

"Well here's what I know so: Mom made the mistake of not fucking enough people before getting married, and she's telling you not to make the same mistake. She's being a good mom to you, and you're not listening, and I don't think you're seeing either because I'm pretty sure Tara's face is a dirty sneaker with googly eyes and a wig on."

"You're eating Mom's pain pills again?"

"Yeah. So?"

"I love her," he said. "Be happy for me."

"No, because I love *you*. And I'm telling you, as your brother and as your friend: fuck more girls. A lot more. AJ, every day millions of people die, and with their last breaths they look at their loved ones gathered around them and say, Oh, shit, I'm dying, I shoulda had sex with more people. But no one ever dies saying, Oh, shit, I shoulda had sex with *less* people . . . except maybe if they're dying of AIDS, or cervical cancer, or were raped."

"That's really dumb."

"Is it?"

"Yes," he said. "It is."

Then he walked out of the room, leaving me there alone in the kitchen, amazed and unsettled by his calm confidence, his *above-this-ness*, a little because of the drugs I ate and the weird-looking stained-glass sea horse suction-cupped to the window. Then I thought, *Focus!* Then I thought, *Balls.* Then I thought if I can't change AJ's mind than maybe I can change Tara's, and that's when I started treating her real shitty whenever possible. I also unprotecto-ed her best friend after my mother's funeral, and that Christmas I stuck gum under her coffee table and left it there. No matter what I did, though, she was always good-humored and forgiving about it, unshakable as him, and in the weeks and months after my breakup I thought back on all this, wondering how doubtlessness like that happens. And I don't know. What I do know is that when I asked my father when he was sure about marrying Mom he said, "When I stopped wakin' up with boners."

*I still wake up with boner*s is the other thought I thought most in the weeks following the breakup and, unlike my brother, I decided to use them on as many girls as possible. I decided to listen to our mother. I decided to have *fun.*

Of course it wasn't always, in fact a lot of the time I felt lonely and miserable, especially in the beginning, when I realized I had no real gal-getting skills and just jerked off a lot and ate snacks in bed. It also crossed my mind that I had given up on something good, something with potential, someone who cared about and believed in me. In the end though I let her go, and over the next few years I changed from a mostly passive prick to a mostly aggressive one, sexing a lot of girls and I'm pretty sure contracting HPV in my throat.

I continued sport-boning broads even after best-manning my brother and Tara's not-as-bad-as-I-thought-it'd-be wedding; even after they had a daughter and named her Marie, our mother's name; even after I saw firsthand how full and rich their life together seemed. I told myself it was probably them just keeping up appearances, but when I drunkenly accused my brother of keeping up appearances he assured me that wasn't the case, then asked if I'd be Marie's godfather.

I was so surprised I hugged him and apologized for being a jerk, and told him I'd consider it a real honor. Then I found out I had to take some kind of church class and turned down the job. He ended up going with Javier, this bible-thumping family-man fuck-faced friend of his with narrow shoulders, and when I went to the baptism at St. John's I was kinda bummed it wasn't me up there waterboarding that baby. And after the priest hocus-pocused and abracadabra-ed her and Javier promised his promises and everyone got up to leave for the reception, I stayed seated in the pew, mesmerized by the sound of the women walking out, their high heels clicking and clonking and echoing in the almost-empty and expensively built house of god.

The reception was at their place, where I proceeded to drink beers with my father, the widower, the new grandpa with the new toupee. We were alone on the couch not talking to people, including each other, until I turned to him and said, "What do you do when the grass isn't always greener. When it's brownish on both sides. Like my dick."

He squinted, sipped his beer, and said, "Leave me the fuck alone."

"Sure."

I got up and tried my best to muster up the enthusiasm to flirt with married girls in flowery sundresses, but quickly ended up back on the couch with my feet on the coffee table with green gum still stuck underneath. I checked.

I woke early the next morning, alone, around six or seven. I couldn't fall back asleep, so I lay there feeling bad and hungry for about an hour, eventually getting up and dressed and finding the car keys and looking for someplace to eat breakfast. I ended up at a place called the Lighthouse Grill, where there were no glass bricks and where I got a pretty decent serving of restaurant-toast and eggs-over-easy and tomatoes. I was about halfway through when this guy and his lady and their daughter were seated at the table next to mine. They looked over at me a few times, so, when I wasn't chewing, I tried to look like I was thinking about something, but I wasn't, not really, just: *Squint.* Eventually they read their menus.

Just as the waitress asked me how everything was, the ice cubes at the bottom of my glass rushed up and smacked me in the teeth, and some juice dribbled onto my chin. I wiped it with my shirtsleeve and said, "Good, thanks." Sure thing, she said and dropped my check on the table and turned around and asked the guy and his lady and their daughter if they knew what they'd like. They did, kind of, and the lady ordered some restaurant-eggs and -toast, and the guy ordered steak and eggs, and their daughter ordered restaurant–Rice Krispies and continued drawing pictures of animals with crayons on the back of her paper place mat. I didn't think the drawings were very good, but after the waitress returned with their beverages she put both hands on her knees in an exaggerated way and said, "Oh how pretty! Is that an elephant?" And the little girl nodded. "And what's this one, a rhinoceros?" she said. And again the little girl nodded. "And this one, here," said the waitress, pointing. "What's this one?"

"It's a giraffe!" exclaimed the little girl.

"Wow," said the waitress. "A giraffe. That's *great.*"

But it wasn't great, it looked more like a dinosaur than a giraffe. And as much as I'd have enjoyed holding that against her, I have to admit a lot of things haven't really turned out the way I'd have liked them to either.

ALL LATERAL

Consider the look on Whatsherface's face when I bought her a well drink and told her I lived on a boat. Maybe my life wasn't so bad. More important, it was cheap, with slip fees coming in at under five hundred a month and utilities topping out around twenty, plus there was a parking lot so I didn't have to hate myself extra when I forgot to move my car for the twice-a-week street sweepers. Also, as long as you were topside and facing the right direction—in this case 127 degrees SSW between the super-hulls of *Fah Get A Boat It* and *Let's Get Naughty-Cal*—you'd be hard-pressed to beat the view: a shoddy bait barge in the middle of the harbor listing heavily under the weight of a dozen or so fat, barking sea lions and some marine birds. All considered, it was a damp version of pretty OK.

But then she asked what I did for work, and I told her.

"I pump fuel at the marina fuel dock for eight dollars an

hour, but mostly I read books and eat sandwiches, or watch my dog laze in the sun and lick pelican shit off the cement."

The look changed, got scrunchier.

"When that gets old," I said, "I sit on a chair in front of the shack and eyewitness the trash floating by on the tide. Mostly it's plastic—soda bottles and tampon applicators and stuff like that, one time a doll head on a stick, another a dead cat covered in seaweed."

She flipped her hair and sucked her drink straw hard, then glanced around the bar, a shithole on Gaffey in San Pedro called The Spot. The first time I saw it, it was wrapped in yellow police tape. I'd go a couple times a month 'cause I could walk there, and every time I did, an old person fell off a bar stool. I was pretty surprised to see Whatsherface and her friend walk in because neither of them were ugly or wearing hospital bracelets. Whatsherface was a brunette and looked like the kind of girl who'd neatly pile her olive pits on her plate. Her friend— who I was having a hard time paying attention to even though she had a sequined top on—was blond and sneezed like a laser gun. I ducked but they didn't get the joke.

"Look," I said, "I didn't tell you about the drowned cat to make the argument that cats as a species are bad swimmers, but they are bad swimmers. What they're good at is murderous rampages. Not only do their turds cause birth defects and mental problems, but cats spend all night looking for small animals to kill. For fun. They don't even eat most of them." The girls looked at each other and made their eyes big but didn't say anything, so I kept going on about cats. My cat monologue. My catalogue. "I'm also not trying to make the argument that cats as a species are stupid. If I was making that argument I'd have told you about my father's cat, Steve, who is a moron and can't recognize me if I put something, anything, on my head. Like I'll all of a sudden grab a can of soda or a fork and hold it to my head, and he gets all puffed up and hissy and gives me this who-the-fuck-are-you-supposed-to-be look, kinda like the one you're both giving me right now."

"Sorry," Whatsherface said. "But I'm a cat person. I love cats."

"She does," her friend said.

"I believe you," I said to her friend. "I believe you that your friend loves cats."

"My cat," Whatsherface said, "Derek Jeter—he's not stupid at all. He fetches rubber bands and watches TV and is thoughtful. And he's so considerate that he wakes me in the morning by gently pawing my face." She went on to list more supposed-to-be-considerate things Derek Jeter did and said something about natural survival instincts, but I got distracted by her friend glinting her way toward the bathroom like a Sparkletts water truck.

". . . and that's why there are so many strays," she said.

"There are so many strays 'cause cats fuck a lot and my friend's tabby got cut in half by the parking garage gate in his apartment complex—how's that for survival instincts?" She was so horrified that it was kind of great, but I knew I was blowing any chance I had with her, so I did the only thing I could do—I tried to change the subject.

"He kept its body in a shoebox in his fridge for a week so his crazy Guamanian girlfriend could say her teary goodbyes when she got home from her business trip. I mean, imagine that," I said, "having to choke back the weepies every time you need to cream your coffee or butter your toast. Or do you not refrigerate your butter?"

I swirled my drink and watched the bubbles spin and gather at the top where they looked like fish eggs. Then I put it back down, waiting for her answer, but she didn't have anything to say about butter or cats or anything else about anything after that, at least not to me. And when her friend came out of the bathroom the two of them whispered to each other and, feeling left out and vindictive, I leaned in and asked the shiny one if her shirt came with matching ice skates. She looked confused, then figured it out and slivered her eyes at me. I smiled dumbly, but it was too late for that because they stood up and left without saying goodbye. I waved at the back of their heads, and then at Johnny with the neck tattoo that looked more like a butthole than a gunshot. When he finally came over I ordered a double something from him, cheers-ed to cat shit everywhere and said bye-bye to myself—"bye-bye"— and drank it down.

In the morning I was back on the dock again, feeling like trash again, watching the trash flotilla again, which was usually pretty big in the summer 'cause there's a lot more people on boats and beaches in the summer, but it was overcast and cool that morning, June gloom in July, so there wasn't much to see until the yacht club kids sailed past in little racers to practice their tacking and buoy-rounding. I rolled up my shirtsleeves and watched from my chair for a while, until some shithead in a shiny new Bayliner came barreling up the channel and smashed into the dock and got all angry with me for not holding

his two tons of bad taste off the bulkhead bare-handed. By the
time I got him tied off he was already on the dock and squatting, running his fingers along a six-inch gouge.

"Look at this," he said.

So I looked at it.

"Fuck," he said. "It's all fucked up now."

Then he looked at me, expectantly, like, Say something, so
I said something. I said: "What octane?"

He stared at me and shook his head but didn't leave, I
think because somewhere deep down in his shithead heart
he knew he was clueless and just putting on a show for the
woman who was on deck holding a rope looking confused
and scared and besides, we had the cheapest fuel in the harbor.
It's a true fact: our gallons were a good ten cents less than Mike's
in the main channel, and everybody around knew it.

The guy was still sputtering in mock disbelief when the
woman interrupted. "Look at *him*," she said, trying to break
the tension. "He's got a tongue like a necktie. That a French
bulldog?"

"Mostly," I said. "That's Jason. He likes garage sales and bird
shit."

She laughed in that singsongy feminine way, high-pitched
and sincere, and it made me like her. She all of a sudden reminded
me of my mother, and it wouldn't have seemed odd to me at
all if she smelled like Juicy Fruit and Aqua Net, crossed her
arms and said, *You boys* . . .

"Well he has the perfect job then," she said.

"Not really," I said. "Doesn't pay."

But it was easy money. Besides the boredom and the occasional shit tank blowing up in my face, there was nothing to it.

My boss Tommy left me alone, I could bring Jason with me, and it was all the free soda I could drink. I was old enough to appreciate that, but I was also old enough to have cul-de-sacs for a hairline and occasional dick problems. My mother was dead, my father was confused, I hadn't slept or shit right since I was twenty-nine, and it seemingly happened overnight. I was young—*blink*—now I'm not. And with all the free time I had to sit around on the dock I couldn't help but inventory my life every now and again and think: Is this it? Eight bucks an hour and drowsy? Should I join the navy or something? And not because I bought into all that *Be all you can be* bullshit—I just figured I'd *Be all a dude with health insurance who's good at push-ups*. And from my chair on the dock, that seemed like an improvement. Most things did.

So when I got a call from a guy I'd met around the marina who thought he was a cowboy and was rich, I didn't hang up on him. He'd recently bought a million-dollar mountainside A-frame five hours north of LA that needed some work, and he thought I might need some work, too, and some time off the boat, just a month or three, depending. "Don't say no, say yes."

I said, "No dude. I'm living the dream."

"Some dream," he said. "Last time I saw you, you were holding a bottle of your own urine."

"I fixed my toilet two weeks ago."

"Well that's why I'm asking you up here," he said. "You're handy and accustomed to the less-than-ideal. Just think of it—"

"Appreciate the offer," I said. "But no thanks."

"*C'mon* . . . It's beautiful up here. You'd love it, and I could really use the help. We can pay you more than you make on the dock, feed you every now and again, too."

"Sorry," I said. "Boat's pulling up. Gotta go."

So I went, and this time it was a beat-up twenty-six-foot Parker and it approached perfectly, nice and slow, its sun-colored captain bringing her in single-handed and smiley, then pumping his own fuel and small-talking me and the dog while he did it. *Weapon of Bass Destruction* was painted across the stern in gold leaf lettering, and when I noticed the dive gear onboard I asked him where he was headed.

"Couple shoals around the point," he said, pulling a piece of paper out of his pocket and handing it to me. On it was a list, and I gave it the once-over but the names were science-y so I handed it back. "Every now and then the aquarium pays me to pick things up for them. That's today's assignment."

"Sounds like a great job."

"Used to be," he said. "It's harder to find stuff now and the pay barely covers the cost of fuel anymore. I'd rather be loading trucks for the port . . . Those guys have it made."

"I thought so, too, until a couple longshoremen walked into The Spot and started singing *Ching-chong Ding-dong* over a game of nine-ball. I asked Johnny about it and, apparently, the shipping companies are trying to replace retiring workers with lower-paid dudes from China. There's talk of a strike before the end of the year."

He shook his head, quit at a hundred bucks and three cents, pulled the nozzle out too fast and dripped a few drops of diesel into the water. I watched the rainbows stretch and go oval in the tide, then headed to the register to ring him up. He paid in cash, gave me a dollar-and-ninety-seven-cent tip, undid his

bowline and climbed aboard. I undid the stern and handed
him the line as he started it up, and as he drifted off he ducked
into the cuddy and popped back out with a doggie biscuit and
tossed it over. I caught it and waved thanks, sat in my chair
and listened to the sound of his inboard/outboard idle away,
then squinted into the sun, a big orange in the sky that yellow-
brick-roaded the water westward. I fed Jason the biscuit and
scratched his head and told him he's my little guy, my mini-
rhino, my retarded miracle. Because he was. It was all a retarded
miracle right then, and I enjoyed and appreciated it for a good
three or four minutes before Jason barked at a feral cat slinking
along the gate. It reminded me of Whatsherface and Whatsherface's face when I told her about my job, and just like that
I was back to overwhelming boredom and despair, restlessness
and worry, the feeling that I should quit the dock and put my
favorite shirts in a bag and move in a hard straight line toward
the horizon, any horizon, because it had to be better than this
piece of shit one right here:

Due south was an eyesore rock wall that protected the harbor and a beach for Mexicans that was so polluted they had
to dig it up and truck in new sand. On the cliff above it sat
Fort MacArthur, an air force base from which—if it wasn't
closed to the public—you'd have had a terrific view of the port's
mega-cranes and endless stacked containers, the bait barge and
the always-idling-for-electric cargo and cruise ships forever
burning bunker fuel 'cause there's no shore-power for things
that big. Across the channel was an old marina of splintering
docks and wood pilings that the owners refused to fix because
the city wouldn't renew their lease. Rumor was they were planning waterfront apartments and a theme restaurant I imagined

would serve overpriced crab legs and have Jimmy Buffett on a loop. Another 22nd Street Landing minus the history: shit seafood and big windows, maybe good bread.

I wanted to leave so bad I got hot, but I couldn't leave, not for another five hours, so I covered my left eye with my left hand for a while, then dropped and did push-ups until Jason ambled over and started licking my forehead with his gross tongue. I shoved him away and did like seven more, but then he came back and started again. "Quit licking me, Jason!" I yelled. "I'm doing push-ups!" He cowered and looked at me cautiously, and I felt like a real jerk about it because he had those eyes—half-smart and vulnerable, like an ape's—and then he shot his back leg through his front ones like a little gymnast and sat down and looked out at the water. Then I looked out at the water and watched as a yacht club kid tried to right his tipped-over boat. He didn't have the weight or the strength or the whatever it is necessary to do it, and after a minute of him failing at it, I reached out and pet Jason on the head. "How'd you feel about you and me finding some new shit to lick?"

He lay down and rolled onto his side, then his back, and I stared at his pecker while I scratched his stomach before calling the cowboy back and asking if his offer was still good. He asked why I was breathing heavy into the phone and I said I just did a whole lot of push-ups, man, "What about the job?" About the job he said, yeah, of course, and asked when I was coming up. "I'll see you tonight," I said, "*late*." Then I went and knocked on Tommy's boat and told him about some imaginary family problems and a few real ones, like how my old man ran around my brother's house looking for his lost airplane ticket until my brother muted the TV and said, "Dude.

You drove here." I told Tommy I needed to take care of some things for a while—which wasn't a lie, not really—that I'd be gone for a few months and appreciated working for him, that I'd like to work for him again when I got back.

He lit a cigarette. "Hate to lose you," he said, exhaling smoke out of only one nostril. "Everybody likes your dog."

"Thanks," I said.

"Let me know when you get back and I'll see what I can do."

"I appreciate that, too," I said.

It should have ended there but didn't, because Tommy spent the next few minutes telling me about a chili cook-off he went to before we finally shook hands and I rushed off to pack the truck with whatever and the dog bed and headed north.

The house was a ski-in/ski-out 1968 A-frame somehow connected to a 1970-something A-frame that looked like it was built by my childhood barber, Mario, who gave everyone flat-tops no matter what they asked for. The first thing you saw on entering was a tiny bathroom off a low-ceilinged kitchen, because what says welcome like the option of taking a shit in a former closet or making yourself a sandwich. The whole place was the opposite of modern, a time capsule complete with wall-to-wall green shag, animal antlers above the fireplaces and door-ways, a ten-foot-tall totem pole in the big room overlooking a three-and-a-half-legged pool table propped up by an encyclo-pedia on top of a cinderblock. In total I'd describe the place as a real dump on a half acre of volcanic rock and pine, buried five or six months a year, depending on the year, beneath a whole lot of snow.

My job was to gut it—knock down walls and open up the others, then drag the rubble out through the garage. Every now and again a trench needed digging or rocks stacking, or dumpsters needed ordering or wood splitting, or the cowboy's kid needed watching while he and his wife date-nighted. Phoebe liked to tell me things about her six-year-old life, like how she grew a pumpkin at school and that it was orange.

"Oh yeah? Well I grew an apple and it was bananas!"

"What?"

"Never mind."

"Can I throw rocks at your dog?"

"Sure."

And that's pretty much how it went. I enjoyed the physicality of the work and my evening beers never tasted better because they tasted earned. I felt tired but good, kept my own schedule, was making a little more than I did down on the dock, plus it was off the books and Jason could hang out and lick whatever he wanted to, which more than once was black bear shit. There was a place in the village with great street tacos for cheap, and when I was feeling fancy after work I'd hit the wine bar for six-dollar glasses of dry Moscato served by white waiters wearing vests. I liked to get good and tingly-headed there, then walk to the Clocktower Pub and start arguments with locals who for some reason never beat me up. Most nights, though, I did nothing at all but sit on the unfinished deck with Jason, drink light beer, and stare at all the stars you can't see in LA.

Besides the crazy-making loneliness of it—I hardly saw the cowboy, who rented a house on the other side of town while the demo got messy and kept himself busy with I don't know

what—it was the kind of work I'm good at, and after a month
and change of long days I'd finished most of what he'd asked
me to, the only job left being the last bits of sheetrock around
three large, bird-killing windows, each of them on the south-
east wall of the great room, each of them affording a terrific
view of the small town in the valley as well as the lake and the
mountains behind it, except that there were two trees in the
adjacent lot that were particularly tall and particularly dead,
and together blocked the majority of the otherwise terrific view.
It was these two trees that I stared at while I adjusted the elas-
tic straps of my dust mask around my ears, tugged once on each
of my gloves, picked up the hammer and small crowbar, and
set to work.

Removing drywall in general is no real problem. Basically
you put a sledge through a wall. Repeat. Removing drywall
around window frames, though, is slightly tougher, because
you're forced to navigate more studs and framing and nails, and
also you have to mind the glass. It involves prying and nail
pulling and well-aimed hammering and leverage. It requires
restraint, and I'm not good at that. Things get even more
difficult when dealing with the metal flashing that was used to
join two pieces of sheetrock together before joint tape was
invented, and in my opinion, whoever installed the metal flashing around the three windows used more nails than were necessary. I began to sweat, and it wasn't even hot out. Maybe it
was warm in the small town in the valley, but on the mountain it was a very comfortable sixty-something degrees. Soon
enough, though, I was really sweating, and more than once I
had to stop hammering and prying in order to wipe the sweat
from my forehead with the back of my glove, and each time I

did I'd glance up and out the window in front of me at the two dead trees. Eventually I walked over to the sliding glass door and opened it as wide as it would go, hoping for a breeze.

The longer I strained at removing the flashing the more confident I became that whoever installed it didn't install it correctly, and a little later I was pretty certain that whoever installed it didn't install it correctly, and a little after that I knew for a fact that whoever installed it was an unforgivable piece of shit and a real dickhole. I became even more upset upon discovering—in the upper left-hand corner of the window frame and in short succession—two small Phillips-head screws.

You can't pull a screw, you have to unscrew a screw, which wouldn't have been a big deal except my screwdrivers were in the garage in my tool bag, which wasn't far but seemed it, none of which was the point. The point was I saw no reason or purpose for these screws except to make things more difficult for me, and I stared at them for a while while my ears and then all of me got hot, and I don't do well in the heat. There's a direct relationship between heat and aggression, which is why most riots occur in the summer. It's also why—staring at those screws—I did the only thing I could do: I lost my temper and whaled wildly on them with the hammer. I cracked the window and hit myself once on the thumb and once, on the follow-through of a big upswing, on the top of my head. It hurt, like real bad, and I spun and threw the hammer across the room, then hopped around like an idiot, squatting and big-stepping in circles with my eyes clamped shut, spewing every curse word I could think of until I couldn't think of any more. Then I just stood there, feeling the bump grow and hating the cowboy for all number of undeserved reasons—his buckaroo boots and Stetson hat, his turquoise rings and this asshole shirt-with-tassels I saw him wear once—all of it in service of some misguided nostalgia for the American West. I hated him for his full head of hair, his seemingly easy way in the world, his money and his car and his pretty wife. Mostly, though, I hated him for convincing me to take this jerk-off job in the first place, one that I knew was just another stop on the long line of disappointments, my only real qualification being a willingness to do it. I also knew that—just like all the other jobs—I'd work it until I couldn't stand it anymore, then trade one hell for another. All lateral, no vertical.

When I finally opened my eyes I opened the left one first, then the right, and in front of me, out the cracked window, were the two dead trees. Only then did I wonder what killed them.

I first-guessed it was some kind of tree disease, then got lost on the idea of diseases for trees and then on the idea of diseases for everything. I don't mean the stuff we're used to hearing about—feline AIDS and dog cancers, mad cows and raccoons with rabies—I mean acute bee paralysis virus and koi herpes. I mean goat polio and moose sickness and a flu just for fish called fish flu. There's turkey pox and something called Bang's that causes spontaneous abortions in cattle. Dermo's been plaguing oysters along the eastern seaboard since the forties. Bluetongue's fucking up sheep all over New Zealand. There's a disease that makes snakes tie themselves in knots they can't get out of.

I glanced at Jason, who was watching me nervously from inside a tipped-over garbage can with his tongue half out of his mouth. We blinked at each other for a few seconds before I glanced at the two trees again. I suppose until then I'd only seen them as foreground—as blurred obstructions to the terrific view of the small town in the valley. But now that I'd focused on them directly, I could see clearly enough that they were burnt black at the tops, the bark exploded off in large strips. Of course it was lightning. They were particularly tall.

Or at least it was lightning that damaged the trees to the extent they became susceptible to disease—to root rot or needle cast or canker, to blight or blister rust, to whatever blind random illness you got.

Satisfied that I'd figured something out I headed off to find the thrown hammer, but halfway across the room Jason barked his bark and bolted out of his garbage can to greet Phoebe in the kitchen, the cowboy a few feet behind her, a beer in each hand, all, "There's my guy!" and, "*Wow*, it looks *great* in here. You're really tearing through it."

I met him at the stairs—still heated but happier for the company and cold beer—while Jason chased a giggling Phoebe past the totem pole and around the pool table before she stopped short and stiff-armed him in the face like a little football player.

"I'm impressed," the cowboy said. "Really."

Then he smiled his smile at me, as practiced and mechanical as my mother's oncologist's. Even though I knew there was some false cheerleading going on I couldn't help but appreciate it anyhow, especially when we came to the broken window and he told me not to worry about it, that they were thinking of upgrading anyway. "Some of that new triple-paned stuff," he said and slapped me on the shoulder, more bud than boss.

Then, to make me feel even worse about hating him earlier, he invited me for a short hike before dinner.

"It'll be quick," he said. "Just down the road. We can walk from here."

I told him I had some things to finish up, but he insisted, said all the things you'd expect him to say—what's the rush, the work will be there tomorrow, yabba blabba—and as I stood there considering a response and he stood there waiting for one, we both became aware of the quiet.

"Phoebe?" he said.

When she didn't answer he called out for her again, this time a little louder. When she didn't answer a second time he put his beer down on the sill and hurried off to look.

"Phoebe," he said. "Phoebe?"

"Jason," I said, just once, and he came trotting out from behind a pile of insulation. Phoebe followed a few seconds behind him, a dead bird in her hands held up like a gift.

"Look what I found," she said.

"Put that down," the cowboy said, but she did that selective-hearing thing that kids and dogs sometimes do, and he rushed over and knocked it out of her hands with more force than I'm sure he meant. It shocked her, and she started rubber-chinning as her dad carried her off to the kitchen to wash up. I glanced down just in time to catch Jason give the bird a quick sniff and a lick, and I said, Scram, jackass, and pushed him aside with my foot. He trotted a few feet away, only to stop and watch as I bent down to get a closer look at it.

It was a little gray-and-brown thing with white in the wings and yellow in the chest, its black legs curled stiffly underneath. Only one of its eyes was closed, and a small amount of blood had seeped out of its head and mixed with the sheetrock dust on the pine floor, making a tiny, silvery-white puddle that resembled mercury.

"What should we do with it?" Phoebe asked, still teary-eyed and wet-handed, already on her way back from the sink.

I looked at the cowboy, who was drying his hands on his too-tight jeans.

"I don't know," I said. "Maybe we should have a funeral."

"No," the cowboy said, "I'll get rid of it."

He came across the room, picked it up with a dirty shop towel, and carried it out onto the unfinished deck. Phoebe and Jason followed, and I stayed inside and watched through the glass door. I could still see the breeze ruffle its feathers, its left wing moving a little before the cowboy took a few quick steps and threw it as hard as he could, all of us watching it arc through the air, a dead bird flying toward two dead trees.

"So how about that hike?"

Inyo National Forest is roughly three thousand square miles of contiguous wilderness in mostly Northern California, about a million and half acres of protected habitat for all kinds of stuff. There's black bear, bobcats, mule deer and elk, rattlesnakes and this weird salamander thing, even a few bighorn sheep roaming around. But it was the coyotes that worried me most, on account of their reputation as smart and opportunistic, or as the cowboy once called them: "Jew-dogs." After I let him hang there a few seconds, he added, "I mean that respectfully."

Unlike Jews, coyotes eat pretty much anything, including

dumb little pets that run off during late-afternoon hikes and don't come back. On most hikes Jason would trail a few feet behind me, sniffing away at whatever before playing catch-up. But he seemed extra-excited that afternoon, popping in and out of my peripheral for twenty minutes before sprinting ahead about thirty yards, stopping abruptly to take a dump with this moronic look of worry on his face, then kicking dirt all over it and running a series of frantic laps around a large chunk of volcanic rock. I thought he was trying to herd it on account of, you know, his being an idiot. The next time I looked up, he was gone.

We all called out for him, the cowboy and Phoebe and me, and when he didn't show I tried not to panic. I knew only what I knew—that it was getting dark and there were coyotes out there—but then I knew what I didn't know, because the cowboy told me about a black Chow Chow named Cookie that got itself eaten a few weeks before I arrived.

"This one coyote wandered down the hill," he said, "right at dusk, right in the middle of the road. When Cookie saw it he leapt off the porch and chased it up the hill and over the ridge, where a pack of 'em were waiting in ambush."

I didn't call him an asshole. Instead I just kept picturing Jason's little bowling ball head and his ape eyes, his bat ears and his little paws, the pads of which I liked to pinch when he slept, their prints in mud like fat sand dollars. I thought about his gross tongue and smooshed face, his repeated attempts to dig holes in couches, the look of resentment on his face every time I'd spin him on linoleum floors. I thought about all the close calls: the time he ran onto a friend's covered pool, stopped in the middle, and sunk; the Christmas he got into the weed cookies under the tree and peed sitting down for three days;

when he jumped out of the back of my pickup truck and hung himself from his leash until blood bubbled out of his nose; the earless pitbull he bit in the nuts at the park.

I wasn't crying, but I suppose it could've looked that way. The cowboy put his hand on my shoulder and said things like, "I'm sure he's fine," and, "He'll turn up," and, "There was a mountain lion sighting yesterday."

"You're an asshole," I said.

"Just telling you what I heard," he said. "It was on the news this morning. Someone got video of it near the hot springs, about ten miles from here."

"I like hot springs," Phoebe said. "And the dinosaur with the little hands."

"T. rex?" the cowboy said.

"Yeah," Phoebe said. "T. rex."

"You know what I like?" I said. "I like pussy and baseball and having a dog that's alive. That's what I like."

"Hey," the cowboy said, but stopped himself there, instead picking Phoebe up over his head and placing her on his shoulders. She grabbed two fistfuls of his thick, full hair before sliding her hands down onto his college-ruled forehead. "It's starting to get dark," he said. "I should get her home."

She stammered a protest but the cowboy interrupted. "Don't worry, Pickle," he said. "Jason'll turn up. Then he can come over and eat dinner with us. OK?"

She whined a series of noes until I got sick of hearing it and suggested that maybe Jason had wandered back to their house, was waiting there for someone to let him in. "Would you go and check for me," I said, "let me know?"

"But I wanna stay," she said.

"I know you do," I said.

"Odds are you won't," the cowboy said, "but if you do run into that mountain lion don't run and don't play dead. Just make eye contact and act big. Be loud. Grab a stick or a rock, cover your throat." Then he wished me luck and walked off in the direction we came.

For a while they were still in earshot, and each time I called out for Jason I would hear Phoebe call out for him right after, each time echoing me from somewhere else in those wild woods, each time getting quieter and quieter, until I called out and heard nothing after.

After forty or so minutes of stumbling around in the semidark, the temperature had dropped to where my breath was visible in front of me and I had to hug myself from the cold. My voice was all but gone and my boots on pine needles sounded—for a second, with my eyes closed—like Jason eating the microwave popcorn I'd drop for him on the floor. And so, with no one around to judge, no little kid to scare, I did what came natural: I prayed to my dead mom to help me find my dumb dog and kicked pinecones until I hurt my toe after mistaking an unfortunately shaped rock for one, then quietly cursed my way out of the woods. Eventually I limped onto John Muir Road, a narrow, winding strip of patchworked concrete that switches back on itself four or five, maybe six times. The house was somewhere in the third switch, and I huffed my way up there, my pace quickening the closer I got, eager to put a drink in myself and get warm. Beyond that the plan was to grab a flashlight and a jacket, call the cowboy then head back out.

I was a few steps from the door when a feeling more than anything I saw caused me to stop and turn my head toward the dark corner of the porch. After a few seconds of my eyes adjusting—focusing and refocusing—I could just make out his small frame: back legs back, front legs front, sprawled out and unmoving. I took a step closer and could see that his fur was matted with something, possibly blood, but there was no way to be sure in that light. So I just stood there, unbreathing, listening. When I didn't hear a snort or snore or exhale I said his name, just once, like a question. He didn't move, and I knew what I knew.

In my ears a white noise like radio static turned real low. My heart a pond in a hailstorm, concentric circles of cold radiating out. I thought my chest might implode. I felt thirsty for sand. But that doesn't do it—I don't have the words for the wild vagueness of the pain I felt.

I suppose country singers have tried to quantify suffering—beers drank, tears counted. Doctors and nurses rely on numeric pain scales, lawyers and actuaries on compensation schedules (a lost thumb, say, is worth about seventy-five weeks of your salary). Even poets resort to measuring, be it in coffee spoons or metric feet. So I have to wonder then if it could be better explained with numbers, if there's some equation, some formula that could calculate the force by which my mother's death impacted me. So shattered was my spoiled-white-kid understanding of the world by it that I'm convinced momentum and mass somehow come into play. Maybe an algorithm could better explain how her suffering and dying divided time into before and after, could calculate how precious my dog became to me as a result, could communicate how his loss seemed like a loss compounded, interest earned on a previous injury. Maybe math could help me understand why—after suffering for so long—I don't get better at suffering. But I don't. Every time, I don't.

Of course, in that moment none of this was going through my head with any clarity. Even my vision took on a white, hazy quality that moved from the outside of my eyes inward toward my nose. My hearing went weird like I was underwater. I felt—not woozy—unstable. I put a hand against the house to steady myself. Took turns staring at the ground by my feet and the hand starfished on the wall in front of me.

I almost fell over when Jason woke himself up with his own fart and spun around trying to bite the smell. Halfway through his second spin he caught sight of me, blinked, and wagged his tail nub, then sauntered over like nothing at all, sleepy and dumb as ever. After I'd spun him and flipped him and inspected him for whatever mortal wounds he might have and found none—there wasn't a thing wrong with him, except that he was covered almost completely in bear shit—and after he mistook this inspection for play and rolled on his back, kicked at my hands, and licked his lips, only then did my eyes well up and spill.

The next morning I duct-taped exes on the big windows to warn the birds, packed the truck with whatever and the dog bed, and drove across town to tell the cowboy I'd had enough. He made that face people make when they're trying to divide up a dinner bill. "Well that sucks," he finally said, reaching for his boots. "Phoebe really likes your dog."

"I know," I said. "But I miss the water, need to check the boat."

"We got lakes," he said. "You been to Convict? Unbelievable."

"I'm sure it's nice," I said, "but it's not the same."

"You're right," he said. "It's not the same. LA Harbor looks like the fucking apocalypse."

He wasn't wrong about that, but I didn't like hearing it from him. Especially after he smiled his smile and offered me a raise.

"It's not the money," I said, then told him about some imaginary family problems and a few real ones, like how my old man filled out his crossword puzzle with numbers and tried to make a phone call with the TV remote.

"Christ," the cowboy said. "Sorry to hear that. When—"

"Already packed," I said.

It should have ended there but didn't, because the cowboy told me about Phoebe's field trip to a ghost town for ten minutes before we settled up and shook hands and I made my itchy way back to the coast, Jason beside me in the passenger seat, his head out the window between parking-lot pee breaks and long naps.

It was summer going into fall then, and thanks to that and the Santa Anas, there was hardly anybody around. Most nights I'd lie awake listening to the sound of all the slack halyards banging on all the aluminum spars. When I got tired of that and of staring at the big bolts that connect the deck plate to the hull, or the water stains underneath the leaky portlights—

when I got tired of being tired—I'd get up and walk around the corner to this rundown office building with a somewhat flat and windowless wall and a decently lit parking lot and toss a blue rubber racquetball against it, play catch with myself and think about spring. Tommy said I could get some more hours on the dock then, when it's warmer and busier, when the bioluminescent algae blooms, the kind that lights up in disturbed water like antifreeze. "And maybe sooner," he said, "depending."

I asked on what, and he said test results.

"Finally took the GED," I joked.

He laughed smoke out one nostril and died five months later.

After the funeral some of us went to a bar and after the bar some of us went to another bar and after another bar some of us fell off stools. Others hung around and made passes at Whatsherfaces, but I headed back to the boat and sat on the deck with Jason, listening to all those halyards that were sure to keep me up at least as much as what was banging around my brain, so I cracked a beer and glanced around the harbor—at the lit-up suspension bridge connecting San Pedro and Terminal Island, at the lit-up port and its lit-up mega-cranes, at the parking lot lights and all the stars I couldn't see. Eventually I ducked below and grabbed the keys.

We motored out, past the yachts that never leave their slips, past the gas dock and the rundown marina, the bait barge and its barking behemoths. Past Cabrillo Beach and Mike's in the main channel, the buoys and the break in the rock wall. Past Angel's Gate Lighthouse and the Chinese container ships waiting offshore with their containers and whatever they contain. Past where there's anything else to pass. Out there, away from the land and the lights, I raised the main and killed the Yanmar, sat back and enjoyed the quiet pleasure of progress made under wind power alone.

I sailed straight out, and over the course of an hour or two, watched the coast shrink and disappear over the horizon behind me. I briefly considered turning back, then looked at Jason curled in his little dog bed and just kept sipping and sailing until a few hours before dawn, when the wind dropped into a twirling, seaweedy breeze before quitting completely. I watched the main luff for a good half hour before lashing it down, then toggled off the nav lights and sat at the helm wrapped in a damp, wool blanket and fell into a dreamless, twenty-minute sleep.

I woke to something ten yards off starboard, a green shape like a giant firefly in the seeming nothingness—five, six, maybe seven feet long—moving underneath the surface like an electric thing, its wake all lit up and glowing. Another breached behind us, then another in front, then another and another, until there were more than I could count. I leapt around the cockpit from rail to rail, wondering if I'd drunk too much or rubbed my eyes too hard, then best-guessed that we were caught in an upwelling of the California Current—these oceanic verticals that bring nutrient-rich sediment and plankton up from the deep-down depths, attracting all kinds of life. Whatever it was that I was witnessing, though, I figured I should get busy witnessing it, so I cracked another beer and sat back, slung my arm on the rail and watched in quiet amazement: dozens of sea things zipping this way and that, bursting bright greens that billowed like underwater auroras. After a while I looked down at Jason, who blinked at me from his bed until I made the kissing noises he likes, and he hopped onto my lap where he curled like a mini-heater. We drifted that way for the better part of an hour, and the whole time I just felt so lucky to be there to see it. And when a few of them splashed close enough to get us wet, Jason let out his little bark—which in that dark quiet sounded not so little at all—and all I could do was spit beer and laugh and say, "That's right, buddy. You tell 'em! You tell 'em!"

I'M YOUR MAN

Woke up to a smokin'-hot strawberry-blonde catwalking down the sidewalk with her dog, a terrier or something, I don't know, it was small and it was tan and it was a dog, a small dog the color of sand, wet sand, Caribbean sand, Saint Barths or Croix or Whatever fucking sand, man, you know, the tropical beach shit, and if that's not a terrier then I don't know what a terrier is—and I don't. I do know, though, that it was a dog, I'm sure of that much, and that it was about as big as a dog that's a terrier, maybe twelve inches at the shoulder and fifteen pounds, and that the girl was all slow going in high heels and tight jeans that went up and over her great hips and higher, like past her belly button higher, as high as her lowest ribs even, so high that they definitely must have been designer. I said, "Hi High Jeans," then gave her this look I saw in a JCPenney ad once, a closed-lipped smile with the left side of my mouth but not the right kinda thing, but she just glanced at my feet all icy-style and stuff and I thought this one's Nordic for sure, a real ice queen, ancestors from someplace like Superman's hideout or something, maybe France. But wherever great-granddad was from I'd for sure French kiss his great-looking great-grandkid with my lips and tongue on her lips and tongue *and* breasts *and* vagina, and maybe, I thought as she catwalked all slowly away, I'd even French her maybe-French asshole, not that I'm into that kinda business, at least not on purpose anyway. One time over beers a good pal once said about asshole licking: "Oh yeah, it's the way, they go fuckin' crazy bro, you gotta try it." I told him no, I wouldn't, I'm afraid of it tasting like a double-A battery that smells like shit. He said, "No bro, it doesn't. Girls are cleaner. It smells like grass clippings." I said I could deal with grass clippings and he said, "Yep," then recommended I check out b-holelickers.com for examples and inspiration. I did, and it was horrible.

But I have to admit: she *did* look clean, real clean, like the kind of girl that has a loofah in the shower and runs soap up her cracks and then loofahs them, then, afterward, spends time in front of a mirror with a towel wrapped around her body and another around her hair while she puts on expensive creams that smell nice and have names like Melon Mist Cucumber Time and Raspberry Aloe Hydration Butter, like the kind of girl that gets the Miami Beet mani-pedi special every three weeks at this place called Angel Tips and isn't afraid of the future 'cause she's young and good-looking and has an anus people would like to lick if only she'd let 'em. Way I see it, she's so pretty and has such great jeans that she probably gets more propositions in a single week than I ever will in my single life—plus like five other guys' single lives—so I bet she'd be into it if just as a sort of litmus test, like, "If you like my at this point stretched-out and slightly discolored asshole, then you must really like me," but in a French accent. And well, that's one test I'd like to take, because basically I'm just an old-fashioned fella who wants to have relatively spontaneous relations with an attractive lady who has few expectations and who simply likes me for me and wants to express those likes in the nude. If that sounds like something you'd like, too, attractive ladies of the world, well then . . . I'm your man.

I'm also your man if you like short guys with crap attitudes, bad credit, and a childhood friend named Peter Parsons who drank three supersized Slurpees out front of our local 7-Eleven, then couldn't swing his leg over his bicycle seat to ride home 'cause his belly was too distended, so he lay down next to the garbage cans and moaned until an ambulance showed up to pump his stomach. Of Slurpees. I tell that story 'cause he drank too much and so do I (which is what I did the night before Miss Lady happened by with her pet dog), usually at a dump called the Village Idiot where they have great Brussels sprouts and mix mean vodka sodas for cheap. On my trip back to the front door from taking out the trash my left eye started winking wildly and I got woozy, which happens to me from time to time on dehydrated mornings after, once right as I saddled up to the toilet and unzipped to pee very yellowly. I remember the blackness coming from the outside of my eyes and moving inward toward my nose, and the next thing I knew I was upside down in the bathtub pissing a hot stream onto my stomach and bleeding from the head, which I apparently caught on the tiled-in soap dish on the way down. So when I felt something like that coming on during my walk back from curbside, I dropped where I stood—the front lawn—to prevent another fall and further injury. In a way the swirly feeling I get is similar to an epileptic's aura, only I'm not an epileptic and it's self-inflicted so you don't have to bother with feeling bad for me. Because you shouldn't. And as I lay on my back on the cool grass, the sun-backed silhouette of a bird passed overhead, and while still in my field of view it flapped its wings once and then twice and was gone—flap, flap flap—and then it was curtains.

And then I woke up and then I saw that girl and then I said that thing and then I gave her that look and then she ignored me and then something terrific: that old-paper-colored dog of hers hopped up onto the lawn and sniffed around some before shuffling its rear end forward, arching its back into a position ingrained in its born-brain to take a turd, and right on the corner of the property. I mean, this girl was obviously keen on leaving, leaving me to consider how deep her resentment for her dog was at that very moment. Probly pretty deep, like so deep that if you fell into it you'd at least break your ankle, so about as deep as Peter Parsons's tree house was high, which Peter Parsons fell out of one time and broke his ankle. Maybe twenty feet? And just as the dog's butthole dilated and the first piece of poo crested, it turned and looked over its 120-grit-colored shoulder at me, and continued to look at me the whole time, right in the eyes! Audacious.

And strangely captivating, too. I found myself staring back at the little guy, and what didn't come to mind then but does now is a right-handed Southern girl I never dated, but we were friends. She was from South Carolina or somewhere like South Carolina, like North Carolina, and had the eyes of a Weimaraner that she stared at me with when she told me that as a kid she was afraid of down escalators, and then later and drunker and hiccuping that same night, as we lay like sea lions on her cream-cheese-colored carpet, that her sister was real sick with some girl disease I'd never heard of. I was young then and didn't know how to be comforting—I didn't know how to be anything then—so I said, "Ladies' plumbing," and shook my head, and she just kept staring until I was grateful for her hiccuping and for the drinks in our right hands.

Another time *another* right-handed girl—but this one was from up North and I'd sexed her a few times—she stopped by my apartment unannounced one day and asked why my microwave door was lying in the middle of the hallway. I explained to her that I ripped it off and threw it there. She stared. My sister-in-law Tara stared at me during and for like a full minute after my best-man speech, and my mother stared at me when I wasn't old enough to know what snatch was but told her I was going to look for it, and when I was old enough and told her I was going to look for it, and when I got arrested, and when I told her I was talking to a navy recruiter, and when I came home smelling like smoke and beer without the antibiotics she'd asked me to pick up for her, and when I got arrested a different time, and when I pretended a banana was my dick and humped the dog's face, and like a million other times.

And still another stare that comes to mind now is my father's. I don't know why. And I don't know why this girl's shitting dog was staring at me because I couldn't figure out what I'd done to deserve it, but it maintained intense eye contact with me throughout, and after pushing out each section it shuffled a few steps forward and left, eventually leaving a small, semicircular trail of dog shit along the way. I'm from the East Coast so I'm used to piles, but these were more like little eggs, and watching Jeansie collect them with her plastic baggie was a little like watching a sexy kid on Easter.

"You don't have to do that," I said, pointing at her forehead. "You could just leave it. Also, I like your outfit."

She said nothing, not a word, and usually at this point in a rejection I abandon hope and slink away, but here I was emboldened by my desire to fuck her I guess, I don't know, but I continued. "As a reward for dressing so great," I said, "I'd like to buy you some food." She ignored me a third time, and not knowing what to say after "food" but feeling like I should say something—I mean by this point I was committed—I followed my logic or guts or whatever and what came out was, "Yum Yum."

Food → Yum Yum.

Now, by no means am I about to claim that this girl was charmed by my awkwardness and experienced a sudden change of heart and stopped refusing to look at me and, once she did, noticed I was half-handsome and could tell, with her lady-intuition powers they all like to brag about so much, that I am somewhat talented at stuff and can lift heavy things and am good-hearted, and that she decided to reward this general decency by accepting my offer to reward her with food for dressing so great, and that we went out and had a chicken together and that it was a little dry but I liked the crispy skin

and the rosemary potatoes a lot, and that after dinner we went
for a walk around the cool neighborhood streets and she said,
"The sky is beautiful tonight," but in a French accent, and I
said, "Yeah, it's like a just-turned-off TV—black but a brighter
black," and then we just held hands 'cause there was a real con-
nection being made here or whatever, and after a long while
we walked back to her place 'cause I told her I had to pee but
I didn't really, I was just lying to get into her apartment, which
was real nice with furniture and everything, and she opened a
bottle of white wine with a white wine opener and we drank
it out of mason jars and yabba blabba we played a sex game
called Tiger Tamer during which I licked her lawn-mower-
scented asshole. That didn't happen.

But if I'm remembering right, and I am, when I said Yum
Yum as she stooped to retrieve that last dog-shit egg—right
before she stood up straight and hurried away from me forever, because the truth is I haven't seen her since and don't
expect to—an amused expression came over her face as she
tried to suppress a small smile.

Now, despite the relative ease with which I made my terrible
passes, it's never easy. Mustering up the optimism and confidence and frankly just the bother necessary to ask out a pretty
girl requires a tremendous, sometimes near heroic effort on my
part, especially if you consider all the times in my whole half-
not-handsome life that my efforts have not only *not* gotten me
what I wanted, but just exactly what I didn't. Like punched
in the face, or cross-eyed Karen, or really sad.

But like my good friend Marc, who during a particularly
long pussy drought trained himself to be attracted to fat girls
by watching fat girl porn, exclusively, for months (it worked!)—

I've been trying to expect less, too. To not get so disappointed. To figure out a way where it doesn't feel so lonely. For the most part it isn't working, but every now and then something like this happens. Something a little less than bad. Something that feels like almost enough.

INHERITANCE

"Is this the Sage Café?"

"No," I said, because it wasn't. It was me, on my cell phone, on my boat.

"Is this 971-3415-6217?"

"There're too many numbers in that . . . number," I said.

The woman apologized and hung up, and it occurred to me that I would like to eat eggs for breakfast, and also that—as I was trying to explain phone numbers to her—I hesitated for a second as I was figuring out what I needed to say. And maybe that wasn't what I needed to say at all. Maybe what I needed to say was that I don't know what to say. It crossed my mind. Slowly. Like it was tired.

When a red light turns green, all the cars do not move forward at once, instead there is an accumulation of small hesitations between each car. You yourself might be quick, but the farther down the line you are, the more hesitation you inherit.

You may not even make the light. This happens other places, this happens everywhere, all the time, even in your kidney, and on the grocery store twelve-items-or-less line. And so my clothes were in the dryer too long and now they're wrinkled, and the milk went bad in the fridge, and they didn't catch the cancer early enough so my mother suffered for some time and died. I was the only one in the room with her. Her breathing slowed, stopped, started, stopped, stayed stopped. I tried to close her clouded eyeballs and her mouth but they wouldn't stay closed, thought that was interesting, then walked upstairs to the bathroom where my brother was stepping out of the shower. He was wrapped in a brown towel. I imagine cancer is brown. I don't know why.

"She died," I said.

"What?"

"She died. Just now."

"You're kidding?"

"No," I said. "I'm not." Then, for good measure, "Fuckin' dickhead."

It's been a while since, and sometimes I think: She didn't survive that. And now I'm wondering if I didn't survive that, and now I'm wondering if I would survive if I filled my pockets with rocks and jumped in a swimming pool, and now I'm wondering how small Time is. I'd like it if, asked that question, someone answered, "As small as a microbe's microbe's microbe's microbe's microbe's microbe's front teeth. So small you could fit four billion years in the space between Elton John's front teeth." Wow, I'd say, that's a pretty great answer.

Me, I think of Time as teeny pieces of party confetti, so small it's invisible, fluttering all over the place, all around us, it even goes up your nose when you breathe. I also think it's carcinogenic, like burnt bacon. As for eggs, my mother liked hers hard-boiled, but I have trouble deciding between over easy and scrambled and waitresses make me nervous. As for hesitation, the one that always gets me is the smoker in bed—you figure they'd wake up, sleeping on top of fire.

THE COLD WAY HOME

In September I saw a stray cat jump into the Connetquot River trying to kill a duck. Missing its mark, it swam in confused circles, cried out as the current slowly took it toward Long Island's Great South Bay, which empties into the Atlantic Ocean.

In October my mother offered me twenty dollars to clean the garage she and my father had filled with junk—warped plywood and dull lawn-mower blades, a mask my father bought when he was in Africa making artificial limbs for So-and-So's troops, lampshade-less lamps and nozzle-less cans of WD-40, rusted tools, a rock-hard bag of rock salt, shovels and broken bicycles, an outboard engine with a spider web for a gas cap. I moved this here and that there, swept out leaves and folded blue tarps until I found a molding cardboard case of unopened Rheingold beer cans. I carried it behind the garage and buried it under leaves, hid it away like a fat squirrel and waited for my winter.

In November my father's mother died, and in December he got himself drunk and tried to sleep in a tree. He fell out. You know what they say about apples. I was fourteen.

Then it was winter.

It seemed to snow more back then, was colder. Sometimes the Great South Bay would freeze over entirely, a couple feet thick, and people would drive their cars over the ice six white miles to Fire Island. Sometimes they fell through. On a *low* low tide you could still see one rusting out on the sand flats off Ocean Beach.

And I can remember holding my father's thumb, watching iceboats slip past the Riverview Restaurant. It was very pretty.

But even back then the snow would melt and refreeze, re-melt and refreeze. We didn't get powder, we got ice. Branches bent. Things broke. Roads were plowed and salted but to no use and I loved that like I love a good hurricane, floods and torna-does, the bull goring the bullfighter. I think it's a good thing when the natural world swells up and knocks against us, inter-rupts our plans, humbles our false jurisdictions—and in its wake the solidarity of shared suffering.

Every winter storm AJ and I would stand at the living-room windows and watch the triangle of snow fall past the streetlight, and we'd hope and go to sleep and get up the next morning, run to the radio and listen to hear that our school was closed. If it wasn't, we felt gypped and ate our Cheerios mad and made fun of our mother's hair while she sipped instant coffee. If it was canceled, we went skitching.

Recreation and transportation for the too-young-to-drive, we stood at stop signs in groups of five or six or fifteen and waited quietly, listening to the sound of our own teeth chattering, nylon jackets shivering. Occasionally someone said something like: Fuck man, I can't *f-f-f-f*eel my *f-f-f-f*uckin' fingers . . . But when one of the few cars still braving the roads approached, we came to life, laid claims and danced around and punched one another in the arms. And when the car stopped we ran up behind it, squatted, and grabbed the bumper and let it pull us along a block or a mile, sometimes more. We breathed exhaust and studied Statues of Liberty. Blue numbers. Trunk keyholes.

The best rides were given by new drivers with their mothers' station wagons, Oldsmobiles, Nissan Sentras, neighborhood guys who just the year before were standing on cold corners with us. They'd pull up to whatever corner we were at and roll down the window and tell us to get on, wait, ask, *Ready?* and roll up the window almost all the way. This one guy who everybody called Toby 'cause one Fourth of July he blew his thumb off with an M-80 and the surgeons replaced it with his big toe, he would smoke Luckies and drive fifty miles an hour down narrow icy streets, slide around corners, pull us into parking lots and do donuts to try to throw us. When he succeeded he would stop, wait, roll down the window, and tell us to get back on. And we'd get back on.

Of course we'd heard the stories: Someone slid under a wheel and had their head crushed. Someone else fell off and rolled forty miles an hour into a mailbox post. Drivers lost control and hit things, like trees. Telephone poles. Houses. Pricker bushes. People were killed. Children and young adults died. But no one I knew. The killed, comatose, or critically conditioned people in the papers were from other towns. Only once did I see someone get hurt skitching.

A woman pulled up to the corner of Vanderbilt and Cross

in a red something with a spoiler. She knew we were up to
something because we were happy, and because there were
about twelve of us shouting, *Give us a ride! Give us a ride!*,
each of us gesturing wildly, each with our own two-handed
interpretation of what grabbing on to an automobile's rear
bumper looks like. She rolled through the stop sign and tried
to speed off, but her back tires slipped, giving three or four guys
just enough time to chase and leap and dive for the spoiler. They
made it a few feet before she jammed on her brakes, sending
a kid's face into her trunk. Blood poured out of his nostrils. He
licked it. Smeared it with his glove. Stared at the red drops on
the ice by his boots, asked, "Am I bleeding?"

The woman stepped out of the car wearing one of those
impossibly pink neon jackets from the eighties and yelled that
what we were doing was illegal. All of us backed away—some
on instinct, others habit, others imitation—spread out in vary-
ing directions around her, readying ourselves to run for it. If
she had said one more word, made a noise or sudden move-
ment even, I'm sure it would have been enough to break whatever tenuous gravity was keeping us there. But then one of the
older, braver guys—Nicky Mastro or Alex Tracy, Bobby Ruth,
Tolin Farrell—stepped forward into the white silence and said
so calmly it somehow seemed polite, "Shut up, cunt." I couldn't
believe it, and by the look on her face neither could she. Before
she had time to gather herself enough to respond someone
else mumbled, "Yeah . . ." and someone else said, "Yeah," and
someone else wondered out loud if her jacket was L.L. Bean,
and someone else threw an iceball that hit her in the back.
She spun, wild-eyed and finger-pointing, demanding to know
who threw it. She was then hit with another iceball, this time

in the ear. Then someone else threw an iceball at her and then all of us threw iceballs at her, including my little brother, who really had no talent for making iceballs or for throwing, and I remember his coming apart midair. The woman scrambled into her car and slammed the door, iceballs thunk-thunk-thunking on all sides, and again her wheels slipped and again a couple guys ran over and grabbed hold and got their ride. Five minutes later they came back on foot, carrying the broke-off spoiler as a trophy.

That afternoon my brother and I trailed off to 7-Eleven, where Gay Sal, the gay cashier—who on the side dealt ugly paintings to my mother and other ladies around town, and who years later disappeared and was rumored to have died of AIDS, and then later not to have to died of AIDS but a heart defect—had spread a few collapsed cardboard boxes on the floor by the door. My brother and I stomped our boots, said Hey Sal and he said, "Hey fellas, have your mother call me," and we said, Yeah OK sure, and walked around to the coffee island and made ourselves hot chocolates and drank them hunched over and huddled right there in the store. When we went to pay, Sal shooed us. "*Pshh-hhh,*" he said. "Just have your mother call me."

On the cold way home we were passed by a blue minivan, on the back of it Nicky and Alex, not squatting but sliding along on their stomachs, sprawled out like supermen, the two of them laughing as one of their belt buckles sparked on a bare spot in the road just before they and the minivan disappeared over a small hill. We continued on without saying a word about it.

On Woodlawn we passed the Catalanos' brick-and-shingle colonial with the white picket fence. The upper left was Jamie's room, I think, who in the second grade I developed a twenty-year crush on after my hamster Luigi bit her finger with his two long, too-yellow front teeth during a parent-arranged play-date gone bad, Jamie running home, never to return. After high school she vanished, only to reappear at my mother's funeral a decade and some later, my mouth opening in slack-jawed awe at the surprise minutes before I gave a mean-spirited eulogy that I used as an opportunity to take jabs at not only my mother's asshole family, but also god, fate, the universe, my brother's friend Skip for some reason, the priest—who had just announced what a pleasure it was having gotten to know my family over the last month and got my sister's name wrong in the same sentence, the funeral home, the well-meaning women who said lame things in an attempt to comfort us, the traffic on Sunrise Highway, blue cheese, Republicans, and Omar Minaya, then general manager of the New York Mets. Jamie was gone before I was finished.

On the left was Tommy Decosta's, who would eventually pull his police-issued pistol and point it at my face over a drunk misunderstanding on a humid summer night, and who, to my own surprise, I would walk directly toward, screaming.

We passed the Scheiblers' white single-story, the quiet couple who never had kids, and then the yellow house where the Gimmlers did and beat them until one day there were moving trucks outside and they were all gone forever.

Lastly was the McMillans', a family of right-winger lawn-care nuts I never liked much in the way a kid can not like someone but not know why until they're older, and then I just

felt bad about not liking them when, after the funeral, the
Mrs. brought us trays and trays of lasagnas and zitis and cas-
seroles, all of us drinking more than eating anyway.

Then my brother and I were home.

Before heading inside we checked the bashed-in metal mailbox with no number because checking the bashed-in metal mailbox with no number for mail was exciting even though we
never got any, then we walked around the house to the back
door. When we reached it I didn't go in, instead I turned and
made for the garage. My brother followed for a ways, then
stopped and—just before I rounded the far corner—yelled,
"Look! I'm peeing hydrochloric acid!" Yeah-yeah, sure, I said.
"No seriously! Look, it's smoking!"

The temperature had risen to just above freezing, and the
icicles hanging from the garage roof had begun to melt and
dripped a straight line of different-sized holes in the snow,
and I hovered above them for a second, marveling at them
like tiny crop circles. Then I kicked around with my boots
till I found the Rheingold cans, picked one up and took my
right glove off and pulled the tab. The first sip was slushy and
bitter and I retched and spit. The second sip was the same,
only I pinched my nose to kill the taste and kept it down.

I looked toward the house, where through the window
I could see my mother cooking dinner, the long twisty cord of
the phone stretched across the kitchen as she wooden-spooned
something around the hundred-plus-year-old iron pan she'd
inherited, the same pan my father would eventually ruin with
soap and steel wool, making my mother cry for the thousandth

time. Most likely he'd be on the couch in front of the TV in the den—the same couch he'd sleep on for a year and a half after she died—his shirt pocket filled with pretzels he'd snuck in there, a half-completed crossword in his lap. My sister would for sure be upstairs in her room doing who knows what, daydreaming of Bon Jovi probably, and my brother would still be in the hallway, defrosting himself over the radiator, dripping snow while our overweight bulldog Roxy came up wiggling her whole body to greet him, grunting like a pig as she licked the puddles forming at his feet. They were all there and they were waiting for me, and we were going to have dinner together and tell one another stories from our great day.

But for right then I was still fourteen and drinking my first and then second beer behind the garage, thrilled at this new feeling—a feeling not unlike the slippery happiness of being dragged along by something larger than me—as I watched the house and dreamed of my family inside it. And as if I'd conjured them, there they were in the bay window, all of them, gathering in the dining room for whatever my mother had cooked us for dinner. I watched them and drank, and just as everything was starting to feel soft and warm the wind gusted the snow sideways off the roof and the pine trees and the ground, whirling the world white.

OK

This is the one where I AmEx-ed my way from California to Ohio to see Fatlegs after she headfirsted her way into the world and forever ruined Tara's vagina—that's what my brother says anyway, and he would know, he's seen it—me calling her Fatlegs cause she had fat legs and 'cause I'm not clever. When he put her in my arms for the first time I couldn't help but be amazed at how little she was, and loud, and then I was disgusted when he told me the details of the delivery as he sipped his bottle of Budweiser, me in my head recalling that smart thing a smart person once said about birth: *Between shit and piss we are born* . . . but in Latin! "Yep," I said to myself, then, "Yep, yep, yippeeeeeeeee," as I pinched her fat legs and poked her tummy and touched her nose before handing her back to my brother and grabbing myself a beer, the first of many that trip, 'cause Fatlegs was something to celebrate and 'cause that visit was followed by another—which is what this is really all

about—a four-day reconnaissance mission to 3 Woodlawn
Avenue on Long Island to check how bad things had gotten
with my father.

Bad.

I stood there wondering mostly about the toaster, unplugged
and finger-smudged and tipped over on the old mail– and crumb-
covered counter, both slots duct-taped shut for a reason or reasons I couldn't figure. I gave up to consider the microwave, its
once-white touch pad brown with index-finger grime, the handle
a few shades darker, a wire coat hanger dangling from it, dis-
playing a half dozen different rubber bands and a Looney Tunes
necktie. It was his Christmas one, Bugs Bunny busting out of a
gift box holding a candy-cane-colored carrot and looking that
look he looks before he asks that thing he asks, and me in my
head again answering that I have no idea what's up, because I
didn't. It was ninety-something and humid, seven and some
months since last December when we all got together at my
sister's place and ate pot cookies and drove through the car wash
three times until Dad thought he was having a heart attack. We
were headed to the hospital but got hamburgers instead.

I put my bags down to scratch my itching ankles, the fleas
pinging and ponging off them as I dirty-looked the three U.S.
Postal baskets under the table on the filthy floor, the first filled
with newspapers and crossword books, another with electrical
cables and old batteries, the third with empty bottles of diet cola
and cranberry juice. I worried about his urethra while getting
hypnotized by the refrigerator-freezer, the only clean-looking
thing around, now magnet-and-picture-less. I supposed he
was trying to forget us, and I supposed I was there to remind
him.

But he was at work for another hour or so, so I double-
timed it up the stairs and into the bathroom where I found
Steve on top of the toilet tank, skinny and unmoving and staring into the corner at something only he could see, a yellowed
flea collar too tight around his narrow neck. He was relatively
new, a supposed-to-be-low-maintenance pet my brother res-
cued to keep our father company and help him along. I cat-
called him like *psssssswsssswssssss*, hi Steve, hey boy, then
reached out to pet him but he got all puffed up and hissy and
clawed the air near my hand like an asshole, so I called him an
asshole and a fuckface and tried to pet him again, because now
it was a thing between us, a competition, a cat-petting one. "I'm
gonna fuckin' pet you, dude," I said. But this time he bolted
off the tank and into the tub where he stood his ground, high-
pitch-noising at me and shadowboxing the air whenever I
got too close. "OK, you little jerk," I said. Then I turned on
the shower.

Would anyone believe me if I said that didn't work, that he
didn't leave? Because that's what I'm saying: that didn't work
and he didn't leave. He only flinched a little and blinked a lot
at the offending water, and I was frightened by this wet thing
looking at me all mad and drippy. I'd never seen a cat do anything like that before, and I tried to imagine what exactly has
to happen to a cat to make it behave this way. I don't know,
and am disappointed in my brain's failure to conjure anything
except the memory of my father crawling around in his purple
underwear the night my mother died, one-legged and drunk as
hell as he made his sad and slow way across the floor to the
bathroom.

What my brain *could* do though was realize just how

skinny Steve was now that he was wet, really skinny, and I prodded him with the business end of the toilet plunger to scoot him to the far end of the tub, then stripped down and climbed in with him, at the opposite end, to cool down and think, and the first thing I thought was how much I hated the second shower curtain.

The reason there were two: some years back, like twelve years back, water started coming through the hallway ceiling below. My father put a second shower curtain against the wall and over the window as a stopgap, he said, until he could get the rotting wood windowsill replaced and the tub re-caulked. Only he never did. There was a great deal of infighting about it until he agreed to hire somebody, only he kept putting it off by not being around when the guy showed up.

The guy finally got his chance some Sunday by dropping by unexpectedly after the ten o'clock at St. John's the Episcopal, his entire family in tow. My father told me he looked out the window and saw three Mexican women and an unidentified dude eating corn while four kids took one-a-time turns jumping off the porch and throwing pinecones at a fifth. I was just happy to hear it was being fixed, only to discover on my next visit home it wasn't. My father didn't pay the guy to replace the caulking or the sill. He paid him to install a suspended ceiling under the damaged one in the hall, the foam-tile kind with the drop-down metal grid you see in dentists' offices and commercial properties.

"That way when the water leaks I can just replace the tiles," is what he told us.

The second shower curtain was a reminder of all that, and by default a reminder of all the other repair jobs he fucked up

or sabotaged; the end table propped up with a tennis ball on a
Snapple bottle, the vise grips for a sink hot-water handle, the
boats he left to leaf litter and long winters. And it was this, the
boats he neglected to winterize—leaving two to ice over and
sink and another's engine block to crack—that injured me more
than anything. My happiest years were the ones I spent on those
boats, dicking around the river with pals or zipping across the
flat and glassy bay at five a.m. to surf the sandbar off Sunken
Forest before the wind got on it, then foot-clamming for lunch.
There were fishing trips and camping trips and rides up the
river at night just for the hell of it, all of us young and tan and
fit and figuring it out over beers we'd stolen from our parents'
garages and refrigerator crisper drawers. The rest was ahead
of us.

And standing there in the middle of The Rest—naked, flea-
bitten, and motherless in a dirty shower in a dirty house getting dirty-looked at by a fucked-up cat—I blamed him. Or
blamed him partly anyway. Some of this, I was sure of it, was
his fault.

After all it was all his, and he did with it as he pleased. But
that was the thing—this didn't please him. This was surrender.
After Mom died he'd simply given up on most things. Still, it
was never mine, so what right did I have to be angry?

But I was, and it was the second shower curtain that
reminded me that I was, and it was the second shower curtain
that reminded me that whatever little I managed to accomplish here was going to come at great personal cost. It reminded
me that this was going to be *difficult.*

I pushed it aside to look through the shampoos on the rotting
sill, grabbed a bottle of dandruff stuff, and squirted some onto

Steve's head who meowed but that's all when I did so, then soaped myself up with it and little by little turned the hot water completely off until my dick got small and Steve started shivering. I stepped out refreshed and shook my way into my shorts and opted to air-dry outside, away from the fleas, where I found and pulled an unbroken plastic patio chair into the garage and sat there in the middle of boxes and bikes and boat parts, that outboard engine with the spider web for a gas cap, and listened to the neighbor's sprinklers tick their afternoon semicircles around the lawn while I waited for my father to get home from work some forty minutes later. His car, a new Toyota hybrid, already had a magic-markered skull and cross-bones on the front bumper and a zip tie holding something in place. He stepped out and groaned his way to standing, smaller and frailer than ever—his denim shirt two sizes too big and his loose pants belted *and* suspendered—and more ridiculous thanks to a new yellow-and-gray toupee on top of his head. I hugged him and told him he looked great, and he told me I looked grumpy and gay and asked what I was doing in the garage.

"You got fleas, man. You need an exterminator in there," I said, thumb-pointing at the house. There was a short back-and-forth about it that ended with him saying he'd just bomb 'em again.

"With what?"

"With a flea fogga," he said.

I tried to explain that that doesn't work, obviously, and that if he did set one off we'd need to be gone for like five hours. He had no idea what I was talking about.

"Because it's poison, dude," I said. "You can't breathe that stuff." My eyes ran zigzags over him as I waited for a response that never came, eventually settling on a speck of sauce on his shirt. Then I knew. "You have. You've been breathing that stuff."

"It's fine," he said. "It says on the can it's fine." Then he shook his head and started toward the house, more wobble in his walk than I remembered, stopping halfway across the patio and turning around. "I don't want anyone in the house . . ."

"And why's that?" I said.

" 'Cause then I gotta clean it."

"I'll clean it," I said. "Problem solved."

"No one goes in there!" he yelled, and stalked off toward the back door screaming at me to leave him alone and let him die already, a tactic I've been familiar with since junior high when me and my brother would go out for fast food with him Wednesday nights and listen to him bitch about our mother being a bitch. Still, his life now seemed so depressing I was starting to believe he actually did want to die, because I probably would, and I followed him into the kitchen and asked if he was still taking his antidepressants. He wasn't, he said, because they made him tired.

"You know dead is like being super tired forever, right?"

"Dead is like being left alone forever," he said.

"OK, sure. But I'm your son and I love you and I'm not gonna leave you alone, and if you don't hire a fuckin' exterminator I'm gonna keep you on life support for a decade and invite people over to the house every day. Friends, enemies, the fuckin' mailman . . . I'll put up a sign in 7-Eleven that says, Hey, Everybody, come over. And when everybody comes over, you know what they'll see? They'll see a very clean house and another sign with the word *asshole* on it, with an arrow

pointing to your fuckin' face, and next to that I'll hang a picture of your actual asshole—'cause I'll be able to take one
when you're in your coma—and then we'll all play a game of
Photo Hunt that no one will win because they won't see a
fuckin' difference you asshole."

"I don't want strangers in here!"

"I realize that," I said, and watched him dig through his
pockets and drop pennies into a margarine container filled
with coins and old keys, the old keys bothering me in a way I
have trouble articulating. Not then but weeks later I would
tell this to my sister and wonder aloud if it's possible to reverse-
engineer locks for them, and Jackie would say I don't know
but art can be a version of that; the painstaking process of building highly complex mechanisms for otherwise useless keys
from our pasts.

"Look," I said, "I'm sorry. That wasn't nice. I'm trying
really hard to be nice and help you out here, and I'm trying
even harder to not punch your head off, but it's difficult because
I'm pretty sure they're the same thing, you dumb dick."

"Yeah yeah yeah," he said, the opening of his victim monologue. "I can't do anything right, everything's my fault . . ."

"Yes! It is! This is *your* mess. You made it. And now you
have a granddaughter. Do you think AJ's ever going to bring
Fatlegs here to see you? 'Cause he won't. 'Cause it's disgusting
and flea-infested 'cause you put a fuckin' flea collar on Steve,
and no one's used those since 1987 so I'm pretty sure he's
retarded now. His brain's broken, like yours. You need to get
Frontline or Advantage or something."

He stuck his middle finger in my face and left it there and
said, "Where do you get it?"

I stuck my middle finger in his face and left it there and said, "A pet store."

"OK. Let's go to a pet store."

"Great. Let's go to a pet store."

"Great."

"Great."

And we dropped our middle fingers and went to a pet store but it wasn't great, the whole there-and-back arguing over whether or not country music is for white people with patriotism problems, stopping only once and briefly to regard a curious piece of roadkill in the middle of Montauk Highway. The body of the bird—I assume it was a crow—was not there, most likely on the front grille of a car in someone's driveway or dragged off by a raccoon or possum or some other urban scavenger, in any case, gone. One wing was all that remained, ripped from the bird on impact and sent spinning down to the concrete, where it lay glued to the ground by some yellowish-white tissue. With every eastbound car it flapped up, every westbound one down—up and down and up and down—and as I craned my neck to watch it go it seemed somehow alive, like it was trying to achieve lift. That or waving like a trained seal.

My father was nineteen when he lost his leg in a motorcycle wreck in Charleston, South Carolina. That was his word, *lost*, as if it was something that could be found and recovered. Growing up I liked to imagine his disembodied leg on a beach somewhere, tanned toes wiggling in the sandy foam. I even went as far as to write it letters on occasion, the usual stuff, family updates and childhood triumphs—I hit the game winning double; I punched Brian Kalinski in the face between classes and got suspended; I fingered Marisa Muller in the bushes at Bay Road—each one stuffed in an envelope addressed *LEG, Charleston, South Carolina*, with proper postage but no return address. It had been about fifteen years, maybe more, but there in the car I considered writing it again to say hi.

Back at the house I wandered around looking for Steve but the only thing I found was more mess. I went to ask my father if he'd seen him but instead inquired about a torn lampshade on a bladeless ceiling fan on a half-completed jigsaw puzzle on a broken chair in the dining room. "Lee'me alone!" he yelled, then stalked around the kitchen jerking open cabinet doors like he was checking to see if I'd glued them shut or not. He eventually found what he was looking for, a flea fogger, which he set off and tossed in my direction like a grenade. "You fuck!" I said, then fled coughing out the front door to call for backup, Tara answering the phone and doing her best to talk me down, which didn't work 'cause I find her voice annoying and 'cause when she asked what was wrong I said, "This place is more fucked up than your vagina is what." She coughed and hung up, and when I called back my brother answered.

"Hey bro," he said.

"Hi bro," I said.

"How bad is it?"

"Well the house is trashed and flea-infested and he just tried to kill me with chemical weapons."

"No, I mean the toupee."

I gave an honest assessment—it looked like someone glued fake hair to a jerk's head—and told him about the flea fogger while tossing a pinecone onto the garage roof and catching it when it rolled off, but eventually it got stuck in the gutter. He said he'd talk to him, and did, and it resulted in our father agreeing to hire an exterminator as long as I cleaned up the house, which is how I spent day two of my recon mission: vacuuming. Also: sweeping, scrubbing, paper-toweling, sorting, pile-making, Steve-hunting—he was in the basement taking a shit on some fallen fiberglass insulation—and throwing things in the garbage, then hiding the garbage in the garage so my father wouldn't sort through it when he got home from work. By the time I was through my lower legs looked like something the Hubble Telescope captured, a far-off solar system, a distant galaxy, a constellation of fleabites. I was pretty sure I had the plague and lung cancer, so when the ponytailed dude with the mini-keg of poison showed up and told me I'd only need to be gone for four hours I decided to make it more and caught the train to the city to put some distance between me and there, to get some perspective on things, also to drink my head off—which I did in a Midtown bar I don't remember the name of, staring at a jar of olives, and a jar of cherries, and a jar of lemons, and a plate of sugar, and a jar of limes going brown around the edges.

My father picked me up at the Babylon station in the morning and asked why I was back so early. I said it was because I wanted to spend time with him, and he literally flinched. "You're my Dada," I said. "My Daddykins. Your balls made half of me, so we're bonded forever through all of eternity, and no matter what you do I will always be your firstborn son, and I will always love you and worry about you no matter what horrible and selfish things that you do. I forgive you your trespasses, and I hope that you forgive me mine. Amen."

"Knock it off," he said.

"Only because I love you," I said, smirking at the heat haze doing its shimmering thing on the highway in front of us.

"Be a good day for a ride up the river," my father said.

"Yeah. It would. If only we had a boat."

"I got a boat," he said. "Bought it off Wally Johnson a few months ago."

He'd never mentioned this and I thought he might be joking me.

"Really?"

"Yeah."

"And it works?"

"Yeah."

"And it's in the water?"

"*Yes.*"

"And we can take a ride?"

"If you shut your fuckin' mouth."

"Deal," I said and shut my fuckin' mouth, and we pit-stopped for bathrooms and beer and headed to the dock to take a ride.

The boat was straight from the seventies, a sixteen-foot, gel-coatless and oxidized blue MFG covered in pine needles, a rusting can of WD-40 on the dash. A poor replacement for the boats I grew up with but I was more excited than not anyhow. He climbed aboard and started tinkering with I don't know what, making a production out of the very uncomplicated process of starting up a sixty-horse Evinrude outboard, I think to try and demonstrate his seamanship or something, his mastery of all things marine. I don't know, but I went along with it as he twiddled about, instructing me on the This and the That and the key-safety thing, saying, "You gotta put this here before you start it or else it won't start, OK? And this is the throttle, and the warm up lever, and this is the choke," he said. "You gotta push it in here, like this." Then he pushed the key in a few times, the carbs clicking away behind us as he did so.

"Yes sir captain sir," I said, stepping on a stuck up sprinkler head and feeling nostalgic all of a sudden, which I try not to do and usually don't. But this was how it was when I was a kid.

"And this is the radio and the bilge pump switches," he said.

"Yes sir," I said, climbing aboard. "It's *hot* out here."

"And the nav lights . . ."

"Yeah . . . can see that too. Want a beer?"

"Are you listening?" he said. "This is the . . . the . . ."

"What about that?" I said, pointing to an Oakdale Hardware bucket with a crushed-up diet-soda can and a screwdriver rusting in rainwater in it. "What's that for?"

"Shut up and pump the fuel primer, smart-ass."

I crouched and did as I was told, and he started the engine and throttled it up, the Evinrude spewing a gray cloud of exhaust that hung in the air in front of me like some kind of specter from my past, because it was some kind of specter from my past, the sight and smell of it recalling for me the summer days when I was six- or seventeen and he was fifty-something and we were both happier people.

And before I knew it we were slowly motoring our way up the mile and change of Connetquot River without a word, preferring instead the sound of the Evinrude doing its job of propelling us through the brackish brown water, sipping beer and searching the pine and maple roots on the muddy banks for the painted turtles I remember sunning themselves, the painted turtles that would splash down as we passed by on our family voyages to Fire Island or further, the sound of our wake slapping the shore. But there were no turtles now, or trout or perch or snapper, not like there used to be anyway, no crab traps marked with soda-bottle buoys, no fathers and sons on the docks with chicken, string, and net. When I think back on that trip now I don't even remember hearing crickets or cicadas, just the engine grumbling low and dirty, the exhaust bubbling up through the murky water as we went. The nature of the place, as I knew it as a kid, is all or mostly all gone now, and as we motored up the river it made me sad to know it.

A quarter mile down there's a square of white paint halfway up the trunk of a maple tree on the west side of the bank to mark the channel, and my father insisted that I head across to the opposite shore despite it being high tide and the dinghy he'd bought only drew half a foot.

"Aim for that empty lot there," he said, pointing.

"Yes sir," I said, not changing a thing except for my empty beer with a new one.

Another quarter mile down is a small island that was created when the Vanderbilts had the river dredged. The footbridge connecting it to the mainland had been in disrepair for decades, so the only way to access it was by boat or crawl stroke, ice skates in a cold-enough winter. It's messy and overgrown, but there's an old bench in the middle of it you can get to if you push through the low growing stuff, and the only reason I know all this is cause my good pal Marc Bachman lost his virginity on that bench to a high school senior named Vanessa Rodriguez. He told us about it the next morning in homeroom, all us idiots in slack-jawed awe at his daring and his triumph.

"How's Marc doin'?" my father asked.

"Stayed with him last night," I said. "He's OK, considering." It's all I could think to say.

"Sad," my father said.

We motored passed Nicholl's Point, the Snapper Inn, and the Riverview, weaving our way around the million-dollar behemoths that leave their slips just once or twice a year to moor out at the mouth of the river, some of them lashed together in groups of three or four or five with middle-aged women in bikinis sunning themselves on impossibly white decks while their big-bellied husbands drink canned beer in the cockpit of the biggest. I couldn't help but feel slightly embarrassed at the tiny thing I was steering around them as they waved friendlily, one of the unspoken rules of casual boating: wave at everyone.

"I miss the sailboat, man," I said. "And Trumpetfish. This thing's kinda—"

"If you don't like it swim."

"No," I said. "No, you're right. You're right."

Five feet before the piling that marks the end of the no-wake zone he nodded at me, and I throttled it forward as far as it would go, the bow of our little boat raising up then planing out quicker than I thought she would. I backed it down a bit, already feeling better to be bouncing over the wakes of the bigger boats coming in, and soon enough we were free and clear in the windblown Great South Bay, the hot sun shimmering on the surface of the water as far as I could see. I was staring off into the twinkling distance when my father leaned across and shouted, "Where we goin'?!"

"Who cares!" I yelled back, then finished the last of my beer and dropped the crushed-up can to the deck.

Lazyjack's in Sayville was like most waterfront clam shacks on Long Island, overpriced hepatitis threats run by dickheads. But the view was decent and they had Blue Point on tap, and by the time the steamers came out my father had finished his second and become a different man. It was just this total loosening and release from the white noise of the last few days together and months apart. We were transported, changed, all was forgiven. Two beers, a bowl of steamers, and a boat on the Great South Bay. *Ta-da and wah-lah*, as my mother would say. Magic.

I didn't dare tell him how great it was to see him like this, lucid and talkative, not completely awful to be around, because I didn't want to jinx it or worse, clue him into my new theory: he's a better person when he's drunk. He'd quit completely six months after Mom died, was sober and unbearable for a full year until he happened upon a tray of weed brownies in the freezer I'd bought to help with her appetite, then forgotten about in my grief and pill-popping. He ate two whole ones not knowing what they were, drove to 7-Eleven for cookies, and spent the entire night in the parking lot.

"I thought I was fuckin' dyin' *maaaaaan*," he said over the phone. "And it was great!"

I started sending him edibles from local dispensaries in the mail and feeding them to him on holidays, because it offered him a little escape, a different perspective, changed his life-lenses and all that. But he didn't take to it like drinking. He enjoyed weed, but it made him retreat into himself and get quiet. Drinking brought him out, made him social, easier to be around. And here he was half-drunk and happy for the first time in a long time, and all of a sudden eager to get somewhere else, a guy who hadn't been eager to do or see anything for the better part of two years. So, when he was taking another piss I paid the bill and headed back to the boat, him behind me on the dock as I climbed aboard and started her up. He was even moving better now, more ankle, less wobble. How it used to be. The boat tipped under his weight as he stepped down into it, the hull slapping the water as he sat on the cooler beside me, then again as he stood to undo the lines and shove us off.

"Where to?" he said.

"I dunno," I said. "Ever been to Fatfish?"

"Don't think so. Where's that?"

"Bayshore."

"OK. Let's go to the Fatfish."

"The Fatfish," I repeated, just because. The same reason I asked the two kids fishing at the end of the pier if they'd caught anything as we puttered past. The littlest one, a tiny girl in an oversized orange life jacket and pink ball cap reached into a bucket half as high as her and pulled out one small snapper, its silver scales reflecting the sun like a dull mirror. I hadn't seen one in a long time, fifteen years maybe, and I hadn't expected it. She might as well have been holding a tiny dragon.

My father yelled, *Heyyyyyyyyy!* and clapped, and then I
clapped, too, and we kept clapping until she bent down and
placed it back in her bucket and, still bending, waved goodbye
as we headed out and then west, the Causeway Bridge barely
visible in the blue and gray distance.

It was his idea, my father's, his yellows and grays in a grin as
he said it, said, "Jump it," like whatever, like nothing, like pass
the salt. But he stood right after and grabbed the windshield
as we came up on the thing, the both of us saying oh shit but
not at the same time, staggered, one of us echoing the other,
and then him just repeating "shit" when it was right in front
of us, the wake of the ferries so big that my pals and I would
try to surf it on the sandbars off Ocean Beach when the Atlantic
went flat, the whole fleet of them eighty- or ninety-foot forty-
ton double-deckers built to transport people and cargo across
the stretch seeing that there's no car access, and always followed by a gang of seagulls pitching and diving at tossed pieces
of bread by those lucky enough to get a spot topside and stern.
Knee-high, easy, one to two feet, in any case more than enough
to launch us up and out of the water like a dud rocket, nose-
up, the entire boat airborne for one or two seconds that felt
like three or four, the engine revving louder as the prop came
free and out, the little boat pitching left before coming down
with such a thud the windshield cracked up the middle and
the bucket and the screwdriver and the Diet Coke can bounced
out and into the bay along with some other weight we were
leaving behind, spiritual rust but less stupid sounding, the Igloo
cooler breaking loose of the plastic bracket as my father fell to

the deck laughing, and me laughing too as I aimed us toward the red-and-white awning on the opposite shore.

By now we were a real sight, two sloppy sunburned idiots tying up an ugly little boat between a beautiful-looking Steiger Craft and a brand new Parker, not even bothering with the bumpers anymore, my father doing his best sober-guy on a makeshift ladder of two-by-fours nailed into the bulkhead, and me on-the-ready underneath in case he fell backward. He didn't. Instead he got his prosthetic leg up and sprawled himself flat-out on the dock, then lady push-upped his way to standing. I followed him up only to climb back down when he told me he forgot his glasses, and by the time I found them and made it to the bar he'd already ordered fried calamari and a round of Blue Points. I once-overed the menu and added a glass of water.

"Only pussies drink water," my father said too loudly, and the handsomely dressed water-sipping couple to our right leered at us. I smiled and blinked at them till they turned away, then clinked my pint glass against my father's and poured some beer into my warm feeling face. It was good, and judging by the foam dripping off his beard and the high-pitched noise that came out of his mouth, he thought so too.

But the light had taken on a strange quality. The afternoon thunderheads were rolling in so fast it felt like time lapse, their bottoms eleven hundred shades of gray and their tops billowing bright white, their shadows moving on the surface of the water like giant sea creatures. The gulls were floating on the breeze and fighting over dropped french fries and shitting the pilings white, and the two of us were drinking ourselves drunker and watching it all from a table in the corner where

there wasn't much left to say to each other, the two of us drinking faster in an attempt to salvage whatever it was we could
both feel fading, my father every so often repeating a story he'd
already told me until the calamari showed up and he stuffed
them in his mouth three and four at a time. I suppose I was
getting tired, too.

"Look at you," he said. "You even yawn mad."

"I can't help that . . . that's my face. That's what my face
does when I yawn."

"What is wrong with you?"

"None of my girlfriends are good-looking enough," I said,
trying to make light. It was something I read in a Leonard
Michaels story, the reason a would-be suicide gave for wrecking
his car on purpose. But my father didn't laugh, just sipped his
beer and waited for a better answer, and I sipped mine thinking
of one. "Sometimes the whole world seems broken, you and me
included. It knots my brain up in such a way I get mad. But I
know it's not like that . . . look at today. Look at Fatlegs. I'm an
uncle now, you're a grandfather. That's something."

"Not enough."

"Well, whatever it is or isn't you need to figure what you
wanna do. Maybe you should move to Ohio, be closer to—

"I wanna die," he said.

I looked at the seagulls. Growing up my father called them
bay pigeons.

"Yeah," I said, "you keep saying that." And then I didn't
say anything, and then he didn't say anything, and we finished
our beers watching the clouds change colors before settling
the bill.

We checked the gas, the time, the sky. None looked good but home looked worse so we went, bouncing our way across the suddenly not so Great South Bay toward Fire Island, one too many or one too few, the two us now tolerating each other for no reason except history. I snuck glances at him, marveling at the mysterious thing that was keeping him going, and it eluded me as much or more than it eluded him, same as it did with my mother at the end. She was a nurse her whole life and knew the second she got the diagnosis she was done for, then did everything in her power to speed up the process. She quit eating, refused salt and potassium, whatever she could to help her heart stop. But it didn't, it wouldn't, and she outlived and outsuffered the doctor's predictions again and again, by months and weeks, until in a private moment between us she asked me to bring her my father's Ritalin. "The whole bottle," she said. I didn't say anything, not because I was paralyzed but because I was genuinely considering it. I needed a minute, plus I was drinking and eating a lot of pain pills back then so I was extra slow, and after a quiet while she let me off the hook. "It's OK," she said, and squeezed my hand. *Her* comforting *me*. "I don't want you to have to live with it."

At the time I was relieved.

So would anyone believe me if I said I thought it was an act of kindness? Of mercy? Would anyone believe me if I said it wasn't something I'd thought out, that it wasn't an act of high emotion, of outrage, unlike the countless murderous thoughts I've had in the past? This time was different. We'd slowed to a stop, the engine at idle, so he could piss overboard. I simply looked at him there on the gunwale of the boat, the great gray clouds gathering behind him in the sky, his misery returned to him already. My sister hadn't spoken to him in months, my brother was reaching an end point and had been avoiding him as much as possible, and I'd more than once been reduced to tears at the thought of his what-must-be tremendous pain, and in a more self-pitying way, at the thought of my future. He himself had been telling me, telling all of us for years he wanted to die. I suppose—there on that boat, in the middle of the bay, a mile and a half from any shore and with a good wind-chop on the surface—I was finally convinced. He was seventy-two years old. His back was to me. I looked at his slumping shoulders and his sunburned neck ringed white at his T-shirt, the tufts of hair sprouting from it. I looked at his overpriced toupee, at the back of his head. Up and down and up and down against the salt-smelling gray sky like a play-ground seesaw, the boat rolling side-to-side in the surface chop. An iron buoy bell rang in the distance. I thought: It's best. It's what he wants. I should help him. Seeing no other boats around and with a decent enough buzz to quit my second-guessing, I took one big step across the boat and shoved him over.

He tried to catch himself but couldn't, went headfirst into the exact circle of water he was pissing on, as if he was mark-ing his intention, his target, *I am aiming for right here*. He bobbed up fairly quickly to flounder on the surface, the confu-sion on his face growing as he heard the engine click into gear. Then he yelled. "Hey! Hey you asshole! *Hey!*" He slapped water at me. At thirty yards he was already difficult to see, at forty almost invisible, just a head and an occasional arm. At first I thought he was waving, and without thinking I waved back, just once, my hand up high like See ya. Take it easy. Like Nice knowing you. By the time my arm was back at my side I'd realized he was swimming.

This was a man who head-onned a motorcycle into a bus and crushed in his head, had his leg knocked off just below the knee and was gargling so much blood that someone came out of their house and covered him with a sheet. He was in a coma for six weeks and a full body cast for a year, at one point swallowing three weeks' worth of painkillers in a suicide attempt, then woke up the next morning feeling "well-rested." He drank, fought, and fucked his way through his twenties in Brooklyn, NY, before it was just *Brooklyn*, a place parent-supported art jagoffs from Ohio or somewhere turned into something people want to name their kids after. This was a man who was there when it was harder to be, when he would bring my mother to the bars he liked and she would start crying. He worked his whole life in prosthetics and orthotics, a field full of plastics and resins, chemical catalysts and dust—he never wore a mask and washed his hands with paint thinner. I'd never seen him drink water, only diet soda, coffee, beer, and cranberry juice. He didn't exercise, ate whatever he liked, breathed flea-killer, but had just a month prior, at seventy-two years old, gone on a twenty-mile bike ride with my brother. This is a man whose body refused to die, and it was this very refusal—that and the idea of having to explain myself, in any outcome—that led me to circle back to pluck him out of the water.

He was struggling a bit as I approached, breathing heavily and spitting bay, yelling that he wasn't wearing his sea-leg and that I'd ruined it, and his cellphone, and that I was a dumb fuck and a regular fuck and an idiot, and balls and goddammit, shit!, what the fuck was I thinking? Nothing, I said, frightened by this thing looking at me all mad and drippy. I wasn't thinking anything. And then, from some cerebral fold I didn't know about anymore came a joke I remembered him making once when I was kid, him in the kitchen hanging up the phone and telling my mother the news about a friend of his, a fellow amputee, whose wife had just found him facedown in their backyard pool. "He had one arm," he told her. "Probly kept swimmin' in circles." Then they both cracked up.

"What the fuck are you smiling about," he said, wringing the bottom of his shirt out and flicking water at me. "It's not funny. Dipshit."

"I know that," I said. "I know."

The next morning we left for the airport two hours too early, like always, stopping for a last egg sandwich and coffee from the Oakdale Deli. You can count on a long line of landscapers and bricklayers and construction grunts anytime before nine, blue-collar guys with green-stained or paint-splattered boots, everybody shit-talking about the Mets sucking except for us. I'm not sure what my father was thinking because I was leering at a cheaply framed picture on the post behind the counter. It was of a kid in army fatigues cradling a machine gun across his chest, unsmiling under a helmet and mirrored wraparound sunglasses. He was the SAW gunner of his unit, two weeks this side of twenty when he was killed in combat in Baghdad a year earlier. I knew all this because I'd gone to his funeral. His name was Matt Bachman. Marc's kid brother.

It was a major town event, the fire trucks and police escorted the long line of cars from the funeral home to Calverton National out east. It was raining, I remember, and all these soldiers were there to do their flag folding and gun saluting, the rest of us huddled under a tarp together with horrible hangovers, silently watching the whole thing save the occasional wail, the occasional sniffle. A gang of bikers were fifty yards off under a stand of trees in case those religious right shitheads from Westboro showed up with their "Thank God for Dead Soldiers" and "AIDS Kills Fags" signs. They didn't, and a small part of me was disappointed. Emotions were high—they usually are with me—and sometimes it'd be nice to have someone or someones deserving to let them out on. Instead it comes spilling over on the un-or-only-half-deserving, and I end up feeling horrible after. I wonder: What is wrong with me?

They renamed the road Matt grew up on after him and planted a tree in his honor at Idle Hour Elementary. A tree. I'd since spotted his picture all over town—behind the bar at The Wharf, behind the counter in 7-Eleven, above the register in Mr. Video . . . now here it was on a post in the town breakfast spot with the caption: *He protected us, and loved our Deli.* I couldn't believe it. I turned to my father. "Can you believe that?" I said. "What the fuck is that? I don't know what to make of that."

"Make of what?" my father said.

"That. The picture. Why don't they just put 'He was a hero

and died for our heroes. He died for macaroni salad.' I mean you gotta be kidding me, man. That's fuckin' crazy."

"They're just tryin'," he said, "to honor him."

"You wanna honor somebody that's one thing, but don't cheapen it by putting your fuckin' brand on his corpse. He's dead."

I looked again at my father, who shrugged and wiped his hands on his pants. Then I made for the door.

"Where you goin'?" he asked.

"Outside," I said. "I'll be outside."

"You want me to order you somethin'?"

"No thanks," I said, bells jingling as I walked out, bells jingling again when I swiveled my head around and marched across the parking lot and pushed open the door of the town flower shop to say hi to Mrs. Patel, the Indian woman with teeth like Indian corn. She had a wonky eye, too, and I was terrified of her as a kid, but had since come to consider her the kindest person around. She was so upset at the news of my mother's passing she got teary-eyed at the sight of my brother and sister and me walking into her shop. "I'm so sorry," she said to us then. "Your mother was a wonderful woman. She really loved you guys. I remember her at the PTA meetings yelling at Mr. Mauro about the after-school programs . . ." She went on about her, and not once did she spew the usual stuff about her being at peace, with god, in a better place now . . . all the horseshit people say to each other. It all seemed very genuine, and even more so when she pushed the arrangement she was making—I thought for someone else—across the counter at us, insisting we didn't pay. I'd maybe seen her a half dozen times in my whole life and talked to her less than that, and she had said a few kind and true things and gave us flowers and hugged us.

It was the same this time, her coming around the counter and offering a hug and excitedly asking what I was doing back in New York, how things were going in California. How could she even know I moved there? I told her about Fatlegs and that I was here to check on the old man. "He's OK," I said, but she seemed to know exactly what that meant and squeezed my shoulder.

"Tell me about your brother's baby then . . . Marie, was it?"

"Yeah," I said. "That's right," I said, and a few minutes later I was on my way out the jingling door with a handful of Gerber daisies wrapped in crinkly plastic. She tried to give those to me for free, too, but I threw a twenty on the counter and made a run for it, then waited in the parking lot for my father, who not long after came out of the deli and seeing me there with flowers got a disappointed look on his face. "We don't have time," he said.

"We have plenty of time," I said, "and we're fuckin' going, and I don't give a shit if I miss my flight." He fidgeted in protest. "We're fuckin' going. It's on the way."

"*OK*," he said, dragging out the *kay*. "Jeeze." I pushed myself off the hood and circled to the other side of the car as he clicked open the locks. We both climbed in and shut the doors, one and two, thunk thunk, again with the echo as he started digging through the brown bag, the grease already soaking through and darkening it.

"I got you one," he said, pulling out a sandwich wrapped in white butcher paper. "No cheese. Salt and pepper."

"Thanks," I said.

"Coffee, too," he said. "Careful, it's hot."

I took both and thanked him again, then watched as he reached into the bag a third time and pulled out those mini-cartons of orange juice they give you with every sandwich. He handed me one, then the other, and I laid them in my lap and turned my head toward the window so he wouldn't see me tearing up like a fuckin' baby.

The drive was long and quiet, the greenness of Long Island summers passing in the windows. The cemetery especially, its manicured lawns golf course green, the grass about bursting with it as we circled and circled, looking for her plot, my father pulling over when we finally found it.

"You coming?"

"No," he said, and when I pressed him a little he just shook his head and looked out his window. "Sad."

I got out and wandered over to the oak she's buried near, found her grave, and stood silently over it with a mostly blank mind for a minute or so, watching a squirrel make its stop-and-go way to a plain-looking concrete fountain with a single jet of water shooting up out of it. It hopped up on the fountain's edge and ran around it, hopped down and disappeared behind. I watched for a while, but couldn't see where it went. Then I started crying.

"It's the worst fountain I've ever even seen, Ma," I said. "I hate it. I hate it. Oh man, I hate it so bad right now." Then I got hysterical, like a baby, like Fatlegs, like I was rubber-chinning and couldn't catch my breath until I remembered to tell her what I came to tell her, that AJ had a daughter and she's not retarded. "He named her after you," I said. "Kid can't even hold her head up yet, just shits black stuff and cries and it's Marie this Marie that, Marie Marie Marie. It kills me. Every time they say it there's a pang and my heart starts chewing tinfoil."

The squirrel came bouncing back into view, then a second squirrel came out, and there was some chittering and tail-moving before they charged each other and rolled around on the grass for a while, then ran up the tree and leapt around the branches.

"They seem really happy, though, and Jackie's doing her art thing down in New Orleans and looking like a total lesbo like, you know, when girls are trying to be tough but just look like little Fonzies? That's how she looks. But I'm proud of her, and I banged two of her friends a while back. And Dad's still Dad. Every time I ask he says, 'Don't worry about me. I know how to suffer.' I worry anyway. And I forgive him everything. 'Cause he can't help it, same as I can't help it." I searched the tree branches again. "Same as these fuckin' squirrels can't help it."

Just as I said it though the squirrels stopped their bickering, but not before they stirred this crazy-looking thing the color of sherbet from its hiding spot, a dragonfly dragonflying its way over and landing on the Gerber daisies I was holding. It just hung out there with me for a little bit looking like orange and raspberry with see-through wings, and after a while I tried to get it to climb onto my finger but it took off toward the fountain, flew half a lap around it, and headed off someplace else.

"Right now he's sitting in the car about a hundred yards from here, probly eating Ritalin and pissing in a Snapple bottle. He didn't come over 'cause he can't, and 'cause he thinks it's useless, that you're dead and that's it. I'm sure he's right. But on the off chance you can hear me then maybe you can have dead-person powers too, and if that's the case then you should give me those powers 'cause I need them. I know it'd be fairer to spread your dead-person powers around to all of us, but Jackie and AJ are doing fine already and Dad doesn't want help, he said so himself, plus he made your life harder than it had to be. And a little's not gonna do anybody any good, but if you gave me all the powers it could really turn things around for me. I really am sorry for every shitty thing I ever did. I was just so angry back then, but I'm pretty sure guys go through a second puberty between twenty-eight and thirty-two and become pussies, so I'm a pussy now. I get emotional when I see jewelry commercials—it's horrible. I don't know how you broads live like this, it's hard to get things done when you're thoughtful and having feelings all the time. Point is I need help getting things done and moving on and being happier. Also I wanna have sex with more girls, Ma, like a lot more . . . pretty girls on bicycles with baskets, pretty girls wearing dresses with pockets, waitress girls and bartender girls and a black girl, like really black. I really wanna fuck a black girl, Ma, and an Indian girl, and Mexican girls and French girls, and I wanna fuck Japanese girls and Iranian girls and feisty brunette girls, and blond ones and redheaded ones, and I wanna fuck strangers. I wanna fuck a whole bunch of strangers, Ma, strangers that are girls because girls make things better, and worthwhile, and I want things to be better and worthwhile. So if you could stop my hair from thinning that'd be cool, and protect me from diseases and save all the animals in the whole world, also kill my enemies and the enemies of my friends and that's it, amen, I miss you, here's some flowers I bought 'em from Mrs. Patel she looks like shit."

Then I wiped my nose with the back of my hand and put the daisies down, picked 'em back up and took the crinkly plastic off and stuffed it in my back pocket, then put 'em back down and weaved my way back to the car and my father, a process that felt familiar for a reason I couldn't figure until now. It felt like walking through a parking lot.

"Well?"

I didn't answer and eventually he nodded, and we sat there in quiet recognition and mutual understanding of things being difficult for six full seconds.

"Don't worry," I said. "I didn't tell on you."

"Tell on me for what?"

"For being messy and taping her toaster shut. You know she'd hate that."

"Big fuckin' deal," he said, then mumbled something into the steering wheel I didn't hear. I asked him to repeat it. "It keeps the fog out," he said. "The flea fogga fog."

"So you do know it's poison then."

"No," he said. "'Cause it doesn't taste good." Then he started the car and took his fake foot off the brake and slowly rolled us through the super-green toward Southern State, then winded us west to the airport.

We of course got lost at JFK and had to turn down the radio so we could read signs out loud and confuse each other until we ended up in short-term parking somehow. I told him to drop me off wherever and I'd figure it out. He pulled up to a crosswalk and stopped, and I got my bag out of the back and leaned in the window and took inventory of my father, the bumps and bulges of his prosthetic leg pushing at his pants above his knee, his oversized shirt tucked in and his alligator clip suspenders and belt, his toupee, the bottle of Ritalin in the cup holder, a Snapple bottle on the floorboard under his feet for him to piss in. The bag from the bacon and eggs and the crinkled up butcher paper. The coffee cups and orange juice cartons and tiny pebbles in the floor mat. His ruined phone was velcroed to the dash and there were stump socks all over the back seat along with crossword books and mail he'd never read. I tapped the roof.

"OK," I said. "Thanks for the ride."

"Yep. Safe trip."

"Thanks."

"OK kid."

"OK."

"OK."

I tapped the roof again and turned toward the terminal, because we could've said OK to each other forever but I wouldn't believe it, not really, because it wasn't true.

Then I set my mind on getting where I needed to, which turned out to be the next terminal over. I jogged the distance and arrived sweating and out of breath, my shoulder burning from the bag strap as I rushed and waited and waited and rushed, and got to my gate ten minutes before the flight departed but it was delayed. I put my belt back on and waited an hour to board, the prop plane to Philly mostly empty and the flight attendant—a veteran take-no-shit lady with an up-close face like a bell pepper going bad—was kind enough to put me in the emergency exit, my own row. Then we waited, and it got hotter and hotter, and as we rolled back from the gate the pilot came on to tell us we were twenty-sixth or -seventh in line for takeoff like it was good news. By then I was really sweating, the whole time looking out the window at the parade of planes lined up, big ones and little ones filled with people like me, people trying to get someplace and away from another.

I closed my eyes, and as soon as I did the images came quick and lucid, as they tend to when I fall asleep in the heat. Neon squirrels blinked around my brain, and that dragonfly, and I woke minutes later sweating and fidgeting and slumping around in the upright seat, shifting uncomfortably until I noticed a quarter-inch crack of light between the emergency exit door and the window in front. Someone had squirted in that expanding insulation foam to close it off, but it was a pretty shoddy job and the brightness of the New York summer revealed itself despite the fix. For a second I considered calling the attendant over, but after some ankle scratching I decided I didn't care if the whole plane came plummeting out of the sky like a comet. I even imagined it, briefly, the other passengers screaming and flailing, myself unsurprised and blank of mind, smirking toward death like whatever. Like pass the salt.

And besides, I thought, it's probably fine. It'll hold. It's good enough.

It was out of sheer boredom that I started playing with the crack of light, swaying my head back and forth just a little, just because, the crack of light appearing and disappearing as I moved my head left and right and left and right, like I was dancing, or retarded, or both. I was lost in it, lost, until a two-finger tap on my shoulder from the flight attendant offering a plastic glass of ice and a bottle of water for the hot wait. I thanked her and poured myself some and sipped my water and swayed with the light, just swayed and swayed, until my head was empty and I wasn't thinking about anything at all, not a damn thing, and then I stopped swaying and closed my eyes and became very still and just breathed, and a tremendous calm washed over me, an untouchableness I'd never felt before, and it felt good. It was a good feeling. It was nice.

BUGS

I blinked open my eyes and saw my brother's sleep-blurry feet step down three red rungs of the bunk-bed ladder, jump the last two, and thump down on the hardwood floor. *Ta-da*. There he was scratching his head, bending down to pick up a towel off the floor and on the way back up he gave me the middle finger. Then he rushed off to the last warm-water shower in the house. We were supposed to take turns but he argued that I gave mine up by refusing to get out of bed. Why should he have to wait because I saw imaginary bugs on the floor?

They weren't imaginary. I would roll over on my stomach, tuck my hands in my underwear, hang my head over the side of the mattress, and wait for them. Within a minute little black dots would be running all over the place, around each other, on each other, over each other—dozens of them.

Eventually AJ came back wrapped in a towel and said, "The shower was sooooo goooood. It was so warm!"

"Don't step on the bugs," I said, never taking my eyes off them.

"You're stupid."

"You're stupid."

"You are."

After a long pause I said, "So."

He rushed to get dressed and hurried down the stairs to tell our mother I was at it again. I listened to her high heels click the kitchen tiles, click the floor in dining room, go quiet on the carpet in the hall, click once maybe twice between the hall carpet and living-room carpet—the dog had stained this one almost exactly in the middle—and come up the steps.

"You've got to get up, Alby."

"There's bugs on the floor."

"You know what Doctor Grello said."

After a long pause I said, "No."

"Stop it. You know what Doctor Grello said."

After a longer pause I said, "Yeah."

"You've got to stop hanging your head over the side of the bed like that. You're only seeing bugs because blood is pooling in your head. So tell me again, the head depends on what to return blood to the heart?"

"I don't know."

"C'mon Alby, you can't keep doing this. What did Doctor Grello say? Tell me again what the head depends on."

"Gravity."

"That's right. So your eyes are just seeing funny things.

They're not bugs, they're just nicks in the floor that seem like they're moving."

Then she would sit down on the bed next to me and gently take my head in her hands. Maybe that's why I did it all to begin with. My mother's cool hands on my hot head, the blood draining out of it.

ACKNOWLEDGMENTS

Hugest, hearfelt-est thanks go to my teacher and friend Michelle Latiolais, who's been there with sage advice and a fridge full of Fat Tire for just-me; to Geoffrey Wolff for the big wisdom, good cheer, and for shining some of his hard-earned light on me; and to Mark Richard for his guidance and generosity from day one, also for failing out of seminary school. (Twice, was it?) Christine Schutt liked my ugly shirt so much she agreed to read a story of mine, then sent it to her pal Barry, then got it published, and I'm incredibly grateful. Thanks also to Ron Carlson, Aimee Bender, Brad Watson, Maile Meloy, Rebecca Lee, and Jims Krusoe and Shepard—each of whom, in their own ways, taught me to follow my weird.

Speaking of weird I'm indebted for life to Nicole Aragi and Duvall Osteen for putting up with my particular brand of it, and for doing so with patience, understanding, and humor. Also soup. Just point to who you want me to punch. My wholehearted gratitude to my ace editor Sarah Bowlin and all the good folks at Holt for the smarts and the push. Big thanks to Andy Hunter and Scott Lindenbaum, who have been in my corner from the start and made things happen for me, and to Hugh Merwin, who was in it before they were. I want to thank Tyler Cabot for calling my graph shitty and fighting for the work anyhow, Lorin Stein for seeking out new work and taking the chance, Halimah Marcus for seeing fit to forgive my horrible first impression (second and third, too, probably), Ben Samuel, Oscar Villavon, Laura Cogan, and Hannah Tinti.

Thanks to Gordon Lish for the interest, advice, and encouragement.

Huge thanks to the workshop at UC Irvine—most especially to Zach Braun—for suffering through the early drafts. The later ones, too. Thanks also to everyone there who wrote me a check, namely: the School of Humanities and the International Center for Writing and Translation. Bigger thanks for bigger checks to the Arlene Cheng Fellowship and the Glenn Schaeffer Award, and to Don Snyder for the support north of the border.

Now look: When you're an aging single dude with intimacy issues your pals are important—I mean maybe even more so—and I've got a few I'd like to acknowledge both for help with the book but also for being my buds despite my behavior, which was sometimes less than good, and by sometimes I mean way too many times. Marisa Matarazzo, Max Winter, Aaron Miller, Sam Leader, Mike Andreasen, and Mona Ausubel: I couldn't have finished this fucker-of-a-thing without your friendship and your counsel, and I can't begin to tell you how much they mean to me, and thanks in advance for your forgiveness when I fuck up again. I'd also like to thank my fellow Oakdalers,

Marc Baylis, Gerard Lawther, Kelly Thomas, John Chapin, James Santomassimo, Stevie Cohn, Glenn Kleinhans, and most especially Elena Grasmann and the two best guys I know, Chris Conroy and Matt Tricano, who've collectively paid more than their share of bar tabs and dinner tabs—breakfast and lunch tabs, too—and continued to put up with me and put me up when nobody else would. (Thanks also to their wives, Lianne and Sareth, for putting up with them while they put up with me). Special thanks to Andrea Harrison, who's been there through the highs and lows and lowest of lows, and to Beth Haener, who saw me through other, different, highs and lows and lowest of lows.

I want to thank my old man, Albert Walter Sumell, who's a great guy and a tough guy and who I mean to make proud, and my brother, AJ, and sister, Jackie, who I depend on for their love and support, and for having the good humor to tolerate my love and support.

Finally, I need to thank my mother, Mary Ann Sumell, and my dogs Bacon and Chancho, who are missed so much, so deeply, that every time I think of them there's a pang and my heart starts chewing tinfoil.

ABOUT THE AUTHOR

MATT SUMELL is a graduate of UC Irvine's MFA program, and his fiction has since appeared in *Esquire*, the *Paris Review*, *Electric Literature*, *One Story*, *Noon*, and elsewhere. He lives in Los Angeles, California.